The Unexpected

K.A. Applegate

AN
APPLE
PAPERBACK

SCHOLASTIC INC.
New York Toronto London Auckland Sydney
Mexico City New Delhi Hong Kong

Cover illustration by David B. Mattingly
Art Direction/Design by Karen Hudson/Ursula Albano

ISBN 0-439-11518-3

12 11 10 9 8 7 6 5 4 3 2 1   0 1 2 3 4 5/0

Printed in the U.S.A.
First Scholastic printing, August 2000

The author wishes to thank Lisa Harkrader for her help in preparing this manuscript.

For Ashley and Austin

And for Michael and Jake

CHAPTER 1

I swooped low.

This had to be it. Plane at the far gate. Two Marine guards, trying to look casual. Well, as casual as you can get wearing combat boots and a pistol strapped to your chest.

<Jake, I think I found it. Jake?> I circled, flapped my wings to gain altitude. <Rachel? Tobias? Anybody?>

An armored truck rumbled toward the plane. The driver stopped, showed one of the guards a clipboard, then backed up to the cargo hold. The rear of the truck opened. Two guys in hooded yellow coveralls climbed out. Pulled oxygen masks over their faces and unlatched the plane's cargo door.

Okay. These guys definitely weren't unloading souvenirs from Disneyland. If somebody was transporting a chunk of Bug fighter wreckage, it had to be on this plane.

I caught a thermal and rose above the airport. A baggage cart trundled across the tarmac. A jet screamed in for a landing. Guys in jumpsuits and headsets scrambled around, trying to keep the 747's from mowing down the commuter planes.

And everywhere I looked — seagulls. On the roof, on the tarmac, against the fence. Seagulls are perfect cover. Part of the landscape, just like pigeons. Nobody even notices them. My own seagull morph blended right in.

Unfortunately, Jake, Rachel, Marco, and Ax blended right in, too.

I spotted a lone gull flitting back and forth beside a hangar at the far end of the runway. Beyond it, a red-tailed hawk sat perched on a chain-link fence.

<Tobias? Is that you?>

No answer. I didn't really expect one. Thought-speak is sort of like a radio signal, and the hawk was too far away to get decent reception.

I pulled my wings back and soared toward the hawk — then banked and wheeled around.

A long black car shot from the hangar and sped toward the guarded plane. It swung around the Marines and screeched to a sideways stop in front of the armored truck, blocking it in. The car doors opened, and four men in suits got out.

I circled, flying as low as I could without drawing attention to myself. Below me, the oxygen-masked guys were loading a crate from the cargo hold onto the armored truck.

The suits strode across the tarmac. The leader, a tall guy with a bald spot, headed directly for the crate, the other three suits close on his heels.

"Sir. Step away from the vehicle." The Marines weren't quite as casual now. They planted their feet wide apart and reached for their pistols.

Bald Spot ignored them and poked his head inside the back of the armored truck. Either the guy was too stupid to be afraid of weird alien diseases, or he already knew the wreckage wasn't dangerous. Which meant one thing.

He was a Controller.

"I repeat, step away from the vehicle." The Marines unsnapped their holsters.

"Relax, boys." Bald Spot left the truck and strolled toward the guards. Flashed a badge. "CIA. We'll take over from here."

The Marines didn't budge. "We're not leaving our post, sir. We have orders."

"Well, you have new orders now" — Bald

3

Spot squinted at the two black stripes on the Marine's collar — "corporal."

"With all due respect," the corporal answered, sounding anything but respectful, "we don't take orders from . . . civilians."

The Controllers glanced at each other.

Bald Spot nodded. "Fine." He slid his badge into his pocket. "We'll have a Marine colonel here in a few minutes."

Yeah. They would. A Yeerk-infested colonel who would destroy the Bug fighter wreckage before NASA or the news media had a chance to get to it.

I needed a diversion. Had to buy some time. <Marines are wimps.>

The guards glanced sideways at one another.

"Did you say something, sir?" the corporal called out.

Bald Spot turned. "You talking to me?"

"Yes, I am. I believe you called us wimps, sir."

Bald Spot frowned and turned away again. "You're hearing things, son."

The Marines shook their heads.

<Gutless weasels,> I said. <They act tough standing around an airport, but they'd run at the first sign of trouble.>

The Marines rolled their eyes.

<If the Pentagon wanted real men, they'd have called the Air Force.>

That got them. I could see the muscles of

4

their faces knotting up. The corporal clenched and unclenched his fists.

"Suits," he muttered. "Too bad I can't leave my post."

The other Marine, the one with only one stripe, shrugged. "Ignore them."

Great. Marines with self-control.

The CIA guys were huddled beside their car, talking in low voices. Bald Spot pulled a cell phone out of his jacket.

I had to do something! Fast. <Jake, can you hear me? It's starting to get ugly. I could use a little help.>

No answer. Where *were* they?

I scanned the scene. Below: two pumped-up Marines, four alien-infested CIA guys, and at least six guns between them. Above: an unarmed seagull.

Well, maybe not *completely* unarmed.

I flapped my wings to gain altitude. Bald Spot flipped open his cell phone. I zeroed in on my target. He punched some numbers. I dove. He pushed SEND, and I dropped my bomb.

Bird poop splatted over the phone and down one side of Bald Spot's head.

"Aagghhhhhh!" He wiped at his face, then glared up into the sky. "Andalite!" he hissed as he hurled the phone to the pavement and pulled a pistol from his jacket.

5

Oooo-kaaay. Not exactly what I had in mind. I motored upward.

BAMBAMBAMBAM!

Bullets sailed past me. I searched for a place to hide. Something to shield me. Nothing. Empty tarmac and runway. I was a gleaming white target against clear blue sky.

BAMBAMBAMBAM!

I pumped my wings, darted up and back, trying to throw his aim off. It was all I could do. He wasn't going to stop shooting. Until he hit me.

BAM!

One last shot. Then the bullets stopped. Silence. I spilled air from my wings and dove toward the runway.

"Drop your weapon, sir."

The Marines! I thrust my wings forward and spiraled around. They were standing with legs outspread, gripping their pistols with both hands. The oxygen-masked guys dove inside the armored truck. Smart.

"Drop your weapon, sir," the corporal repeated.

Bald Spot turned. "I don't think so." He extended his arm. "Here are your new orders, boys."

Oh, God. <JAKE?!>

Ka-CHIK.

He cocked his pistol.

Ka-CHIK. Ka-CHIK. Ka-CHIK.

The other Controllers cocked their pistols.

For half a second Marines and Controllers stood frozen. Then —

BAM!

BAM! BAM!

Bullets flew. The Marines dove behind the plane's landing gear. The Controllers dropped back behind their car.

Okay. Okay. Think, Cassie. You have to get them to stop shooting. You've got to keep them from killing each other. <JAKE, WHERE ARE YOU? RACHEL? I CAN'T DO THIS BY MYSELF!>

BAM! BAM! BAM! Choooong. Kachooooong.

Bullets sprayed off metal. I swung around the tail of the plane, looking for cover. An engine roared to life at the next gate. A baggage cart, lurching toward the plane!

The cart kept coming, full speed. It careened past a food service truck and ricocheted off a cargo bin. Fishtailed around the nose of the plane. Skidded to a stop between the Marines and the Controllers.

BAM! BAM! Kachooooong.

The baggage cart quaked. Suitcases erupted.

"Rrrrrooooowwwwrrr!"

And a thousand pounds of grizzly bear exploded from the rubble.

CHAPTER 2

"**H**hhhoooRRRAAWWRR!"

The bear bounded from the cart.

"Hhhhrrroooowwwrrr!"

Two streaks of orange and black shot past her — a tiger and a cheetah leaped over the CIA car and tackled two of the Controllers. The maniac baggage cart driver — a gorilla — swung down from the cab. A red-tailed hawk, swooped in from the top of the terminal.

Bet you're completely confused now? Bet you're thinking, *This girl is completely nuts. The lights are on, but no one's home.* Don't worry, I promise you'll understand in a little while. Promise.

<Move over, Marines,> he said. <The zoo has landed.>

<We thought maybe — just maybe — you could use a little help,> Marco called, knuckle-walking across the tarmac.

<And the rest of us were looking like road-kill.> Rachel. Squinting her nearsighted grizzly eyes and bounding after Bald Spot. <We took a vote. We're pooling our money and enrolling Marco in driver's ed.>

Bald Spot turned. Leveled his pistol.

<Rachel! The gun!> I screamed.

She reared up on her hind legs. Pinned Bald Spot to the pavement with one swipe of her massive paw. Clamped her teeth around his gun and ripped it from his hand.

"You can't win!" Bald Spot screamed. "We'll destroy you!"

And then he was out cold. Courtesy of Rachel.

BAM! Kachooooong.

<Hey! Somebody tell the Marines to stop shooting. We're on their side.>

Marco hit the ground. Tobias dove for cover.

Ax was locked in a deadly embrace with one of the Controllers. They rolled across the tarmac, human desperation pitted against sheer feline strength.

I skimmed low toward the car.

<Cassie! Look out!>

BAM!

Jake leaped past me. Claws. Teeth. Gun metal. Blood.

I wheeled, looking for a place to land. I'd started this little fight, and now my friends were battling for their lives while I flitted about like some weird war-zone cheerleader.

I had to find a place to demorph. A place hidden from Controllers. I couldn't let them see I was human.

Because yes, I am human.

My name is Cassie.

But you probably already figured that out.

You probably also noticed my life is a little abnormal. You know, the thought-speak. The alien spacecraft wreckage. The psychotic men-in-black gunning down my *Animal Planet* buddies at the airport.

My friends and I are Animorphs. Animal morphers. We can acquire the DNA of another animal, then become that animal. It's the only weapon we have in our war to help save humanity.

And it's a powerful one, but it has limitations. Ask Tobias. He's a walking, talking owner's manual for one of the major limitations. He stayed in his red-tailed hawk morph longer than the two-

10

hour maximum, and now he's what the Andalites call a *nothlit.* He doesn't have to morph a hawk. He *is* a hawk.

We also can't morph directly from one animal to another. Which is why I couldn't just go from seagull to wolf, my usual battle morph, right there on the tarmac. I had to become Cassie first, regular, human Cassie, and I couldn't risk it.

Because morphing is not human technology. It's Andalite technology, given to us by a dying alien, an Andalite war prince named Elfangor. The Yeerks think we Animorphs are all Andalites, and we'd like to keep it that way. If they knew we were human, they'd find us. They'd find us and our families and kill us.

Or worse.

They'd slide Yeerks into our heads. They'd turn us and everyone we love into Controllers. We'd be entombed in our own bodies. We'd watch our hands destroy the planet. We'd hear our voices spew evil and hatred. And we'd be helpless to stop it.

A Yeerk. It doesn't look like much. Small, gray, slimy. An overgrown slug. Blind, nearly deaf, no arms or legs. Like a brain without a body.

Which is why it needs your body. It squeezes through your ear canal and flattens out over the surface of your brain, burying its slimy self in

11

every crevice, locking itself onto your memories, your knowledge, your emotions.

It takes over. You can't run. You can't scream. You can't tell anyone what's happening to you. And you can't escape. You can't even make plans to escape because the slug knows your thoughts as soon as you think them.

The Yeerks have already conquered the Gedds, the Taxxons, and the Hork-Bajir. Now they're taking us. Humans.

And we're trying to stop them: me, my best friend Rachel, Rachel's cousin Jake, Jake's best friend Marco, Tobias, and Ax, an Andalite, Elfangor's little brother.

That's it. Team Earth: a bird, an alien, and four kids. The only thing standing between you and total enslavement.

We do get help from the Chee, a race of androids hardwired for nonviolence. They've infiltrated the Yeerk organization, The Sharing, and feed us information when they can. But as far as physical battle goes, it's just the six of us.

And at the moment it was only five.

I soared low, looking for a place to demorph.

BAM! Ka-chooong.

"Stay away!" A Controller backed toward the CIA car, holding his gun in front of him, waving it wildly at Tobias, at the Marines, at Marco.

Ka-CHIK.

Marco lunged.

BAM!

<Aaaaaahhhh!>

Blood oozed up through the coarse black hair on Marco's arm. He charged anyway. Crushed the Controller against the car. Whammed him with one sledgehammer swing of his fist.

<Just for the record,> he panted, <I don't like this guy.>

The Controller dropped to the pavement, unconscious.

Jake stood on another Controller's chest.

Ax cornered a third Controller between two cargo bins.

Whipped his tail. Flicked air. Let out a sound that wasn't even close to "meow."

<This appendage works well to balance the cheetah when it runs, but it is useless as a weapon.>

<You'll have to settle for teeth and claws, Axman,> Jake called. <Too many people. We don't need your blue-furred, four-eyed self on the cover of the *National Enquirer*.>

Ax responded by knocking out the Controller with a lightning-quick and very large paw.

Rachel ripped open the lid of a cargo bin. One by one, Marco dumped the Controllers inside, then flipped the bin over so the lid was against the ground.

The Marines were crouched behind the plane's landing gear, watching, pistols ready but silent.

<That was almost easy,> said Rachel.

<Almost too easy,> Marco added.

Tobias and I circled overhead and dropped. <We got company.>

BAM! BAM! BAMBAMBAMBAMBAMBAM!

A line of men in black with automatic rifles began shooting from the terminal roof.

CHAPTER 3

BAMBAMBAMBAMBAMBAMBAM!

We dove between the cargo bins.

BAM! BAM!

The Marines fired back.

<Oh, this is good,> Marco said. <We're getting it from both sides again.>

Sirens. Shouts.

Police cars screeched onto the tarmac, lights flashing, bullhorns blaring. Airport security guards streamed from the terminal.

<Jake,> I said. <They're headed right into the line of fire.>

<Let them go. Visser Three won't want that many witnesses. The Controllers will have to back off.>

15

Back off. Yeah. Except they weren't doing that. Bald Spot and his buddies were rocking the cargo bin, trying to turn it over.

<Uh, Jake?>

<Yeah. I know.>

They weren't going to back off. The police were Controllers. So were the security guards.

It was an entire Yeerk army.

BAM! Chooooong.

A bullet ricocheted off one of the cargo bins.

<What's the plan?>

Jake crouched, his tail whipping. <A battalion of Yeerks against the six of us. Not good.>

<Plus the two Marines,> I said. <And the guys in the armored truck.>

<Yeah, don't forget them.> Marco grunted. <They've been such a big help already.>

<But we can't just leave them.>

<And we can't leave without that chunk of Bug fighter,> Rachel pointed out. <That's why we came. We have to get it out of here before the Yeerks destroy it.>

<No,> Jake said. <We can't risk it. There's no way we can get it without getting ourselves killed.>

<There is a maintenance ramp past the next gate, Prince Jake,> said Ax.

<Good. We can demorph inside. Okay, guys, mission aborted. Let's go. Stay close to the build-

ing. Go, go, go. And Ax? Don't call me — oh, forget it.>

Jake leaped between the bins and streaked toward the ramp. Marco and Ax bounded after him.

"GGGRRRRRRROOOOOOOOOOOOOAAAWWWWWW!"

Rachel thumped the cargo bin one last time, then barreled toward the ramp.

Tobias swooped low under the eaves of the terminal building. <Cassie, come on. You can demorph inside.>

BAM! BAM!

"Ahhhhhhhhh!"

The Marine with one stripe on his collar grabbed his shoulder and collapsed to the pavement. I could see blood seeping from under his hand.

Tobias circled. <Time to go, Cassie!>

<I'm right behind you.>

Tobias soared toward the ramp. I circled close to the terminal.

The injured Marine crawled toward the armored truck. The Controllers were ignoring him. But the other Marine, the corporal, was still crouched behind the plane's landing gear, firing at the enemy. And the enemy was firing back.

One of the policemen held a bullhorn to his mouth. "Visser Three is getting impatient. Elimi-

17

nate the human so we can get to that cargo hold."

Eliminate. The Controllers didn't care about the Marine. They just needed him out of the way. He was the only thing standing between them and the wrecked Bug fighter.

I had to get him to stop shooting!

<Hey! Marine. This is a friend. Hold your fire!> I yelled at him in thought-speak. <Stop shooting and STAY DOWN!>

The Marine hesitated for a split second. He glanced around, frowned, then tightened his grip on the pistol.

BAM!

BAMBAMBAMBAMBAMBAM!

Automatic rifle fire answered back.

The Marine dove behind the wheel, crouching low, ready to fire again.

He'd be killed in a matter of minutes, no question.

I circled the plane's tail, spilled air from my wings, and dove. Under the plane. Past the Marine.

<Corporal! Hold your fire!>

The Marine edged back against the landing gear. He cocked his head and listened, obviously trying to figure out where the voice had come from.

<Back off!>

I circled.

<This is one fight you can't win.>

He looked up. And blinked. "Okay, this is totally nuts." He closed his eyes and leaned his head back against the wheel. "A bird is talking to me — AND I'M LISTENING." He opened his eyes and shook his head. "This is crazy."

He leaned away from the landing gear and swung his pistol toward the Controllers.

It was suicide.

He aimed.

I dove.

I hit metal as the Marine pulled the trigger.

BAM!

<Ahhhhhhhhh!>

Pain shot through my side. I spiraled, one wing flapping, the other hanging dead at my side.

I saw the corporal's pistol skitter across the tarmac in a whirl of plane, sky, and pavement. I pumped my good wing, straining to steady myself. The ground spun upward. Gray. Hard. Tilting. Closer.

Then the spinning just stopped.

CHAPTER 4

I flopped on the tarmac. My wing lay mangled and torn, shattered by the pistol's recoil.

"That bird! Did you see the bird? It was an Andalite!"

Bald Spot. I couldn't let him find me. I scratched and writhed and flapped my good wing, and somehow clawed my way under the baggage cart. Bits of gravel embedded themselves in my bloody feathers. Pain seared through my body.

Demorph. I had to demorph.

"Where'd it go? Where's the seagull?"

The shouting grew louder. Closer. Shoes scuffed past the cart, inches from my head.

Concentrate, Cassie, concentrate.

I focused on my human form. Morphing is un-predictable. It never happens the same way twice. But I'd learned to control it a bit. I knew what I had to do.

Human. Human Cassie arms. I felt my wings growing, the damaged one becoming stronger as my human DNA slowly replaced the seagull DNA.

Cuuurrrreeeeeeeeeek.

My shoulder bones cracked and widened. Wings narrowed and shot downward, the size of human arms.

Schluuuuup.

A thumb, then four fingers, pale and bumpy like a plucked chicken, shot from the tip of each wing. Rib bones melted and reshaped, growing to my normal size. Legs straightened and length-ened, the claws softening into ten toes on two human feet.

And then I stopped morphing.

I was still more gull than girl, a weird mix of fluffy wings and pure horror. The Blair Muppet Project. But I didn't look human. Not even close.

I inched out from under the baggage cart. Controllers were storming the cargo hold of the plane, closing off the entire area. Tobias and the others were long gone, but I could see the main-tenance ramp they'd escaped into at the next gate.

And I had a clear shot. Nobody was paying

any attention to the giant mutant seagull crouched beside the baggage cart.

I pulled myself up and ran, full out, almost human arms still covered in feathers, almost human feet slapping the pavement under scaly Big Bird legs, my own short dark hair looking more than a little strange on my giant seagull head.

I veered in toward the terminal building, stayed beneath its shadow. Past the first gate. Followed the curve of the building. The next gate was dead ahead.

"There it is!"

Bald Spot! Behind me.

"Stop the Andalite filth before it gets away!"

The ramp was just a few yards ahead. I could make it. I was going to make it!

Ka-CHIK.

A glint of gun metal. A police Controller stepped out from behind a cargo bin, directly between me and the ramp. I turned. Bald Spot circled wide to cut me off. I turned again, back to the baggage cart. Controllers raced toward me on the other side. I was trapped. Me and the baggage cart, surrounded by Controllers.

I whirled. No way out.

No — one way out. The Marco way.

I scrambled into the cart, turned the key, and floored it.

The cart jerked, stopped, then lurched forward at full throttle, throwing me back against the seat. Bald Spot dove to the pavement as I shot past. I grabbed the wheel and tried to steer, a grotesque seagull-like thing the size of a kid, screeching through the airport on two wheels.

I sped under the wing of the plane and swerved, sideswiping the landing gear. Luggage spilled from the back of the cart. I swung the wheel around and headed out toward the open tarmac. If I got out of there alive, I'd never again give Marco a hard time about his driving. He was Jeff Gordon compared to me.

Sirens. Flashing red and blue lights.

I whipped my bird head around. Two police cars behind me. In seconds they'd be within firing range.

I jerked the wheel and rocketed toward one of the planes. Under the wing. Around the wheels. Between two rows of cargo.

I hurtled around a food service truck and glanced back. I'd gained a little ground. The police cars were a lot bigger than my suitcase-mobile. They swung wide of the jet, while I plowed straight underneath.

I headed toward the next gate, and then the next. In. Out. Under. Around. Getting the hang of the steering thing.

23

The Controllers roared past.

A 747, looming ahead! Not a problem. I gripped the wheel and sped straight toward it. Under the engines, around the front wheels. I could see the corner of the terminal building as I whipped past.

Shot out from under the nose of the 747 —

Straight onto open tarmac! Two police cars barreled toward me. In a split second I'd plow into them, head-on.

I jerked the wheel and skidded into a tight U. Tires squeeled. More suitcases flew.

I looked back. A garment bag flapped onto the windshield of one of the police cars. Nice. The car screeched one way, then another, as the driver leaned out the window, trying to grab the bag off the windshield. The other car veered toward the runway to keep from getting creamed.

Okay. That bought me a little more time. But I couldn't race through the airport forever. I had to find a place to finish demorphing, then morph something that could get out of there.

Ahead, a set of roll-away stairs pushed up to the door of a jet. Guys in orange jumpsuits dragging buckets and a shop vac down the steps. A cleaning crew! The plane was probably empty. I raced toward it.

A siren wailed behind me.

The cleaning crew had reached the tarmac.

Started to roll the steps away from the plane. I turned the wheel and tried to find the brake. The cart skidded sideways. The cleaning crew scattered, buckets flying as they dove for cover. I hammered the pedals with my feet, but the cart wouldn't slow down!

Ssscccrrrrrnnnnnnnncchhhh-KUUUNNNKK.

I crashed into the stairs. My bird-girl body snapped forward against the steering wheel, then back against the seat.

Oh. Ow. I swallowed. Brakes would have been easier, but the head-on collision had worked.

No time to catch my breath. I bolted from the baggage cart and up the steps. The impact from the crash had jerked the stairs several feet from the door of the plane, but I didn't let a 12-foot drop stop me. I hurdled the gap and landed with a soft thunk on the thin carpeting inside the plane.

Police lights flashed through the door of the cabin. I peeled myself from the floor and ran.

WHUMP!

The entire plane shuddered as the roll-away stairs banged against the cabin door. I tore down the aisle, looking for a place to demorph. I could hear shouting below me, footsteps clanking up the stairs.

"This way! Over here!"

"The Andalite's inside!"

I'd reached the back of the plane. Hide. I had to hide!

I whirled. Seats. Baggage compartments. A door handle! I lunged for it and pushed. The bathroom.

I fell inside and bolted the door.

CHAPTER 5

Demorph. Fast!

I could hear Controllers thundering onto the plane.

Focus, Cassie, focus. You have to reverse this morph.

I felt my body becoming heavier as my hollow bird bones thickened into solid human skeleton. My feathers darkened and dissolved, the plucked bird skin underneath smoothing into brown skin.

Cuuurrrrrruuuunnnch.

My jaw pushed out from my remolded skull. Tailbone shrank up into my spine. I was almost human now, fully human, except for the enormous seagull beak jutting from my face.

"Where'd it go?"

"The cockpit! Check the cockpit."

I held my hands over my ears and concentrated.

The beak softened and melted into my face. Two lips. A nose. I was human.

But I couldn't stay that way.

I dropped into the cramped space beside the toilet and the sink. The metal of the sink was so cool and smooth. I lay my face against it. If I could just stay there a minute and —

"The Andalite has to be here. FIND IT!"

I jerked my head up. *Snap out of it, Cassie.* I fixed my mind on fly morph.

Sploooot. Sploooot.

A pair of antennae shot out my forehead.

Pop. Pop-pop. Pop-pop-pop-pop-pop.

Stiff black hairs popped out like zits all over my body. Two tissue-thin wings emerged from my back.

"Nothing in the cockpit."

"Or the galley."

I could hear Controllers tearing through the cabin of the plane. Footsteps. Shouts. Ripped seat cushions.

Relax, Cassie. Think fly.

A pair of black nubs pushed out from my sides, writhing into long hairy fly legs. My own arms and legs thinned and hardened. Hands and feet shriveled into sticky claws.

The door handle rattled. "It's locked!"

"Good. We've found the Andalite scum."

Concentrate. Fly. Small. SMALL. Speed it up!

The floor zoomed up at me as my body shrank to the size of a bread crumb.

BAM! BAM! Clink. Ka-Clink.

Bullets flew through the thin metal of the door and ricocheted off the sink. The sink that now towered above me. The sink that shattered into thousands of sinks as my human eyes bulged out into compound fly eyes.

Ssshhhlllllluuuuuuulp.

Bones dissolved. Skin darkened and hardened into a shiny, crisp coating over the bulging fly body.

Sssssuuuuuummmmp. Sproot-sproot.

My lips sprouted down into the fly's snout-shaped proboscis. Two spongy bumps erupted at the end. I was fly now. Pure fly. A fly in fly heaven. A bathroom. Each tiny black hair on my body quivered in delight. Through the stench of disinfectant cleanser, I could detect the glorious aroma of —

BAM! BAM! Ka-Clink.

Whoa. Time to get a grip on the fly instincts. I buzzed into the little space between the rim of the toilet bowl and the seat. As soon as the door opened I'd zoom out.

BAM! Ka-Clink.

"I can shoot the lock off."

"And give the Andalite a chance to escape?"

"But it's gotta be dead. The door is Swiss cheese."

"And you think that Andalite let us shoot him? Idiot! It probably morphed an insect. We'll have to gas it."

Gas! I buzzed around the tiny bathroom, looking for a way out. The sink! I could fly down the drain. I shot into the metal basin.

Tlink.

<Agggghhh.>

A stupid airplane sink with a stupid sliding metal plate over the drain! A plate no housefly could ever hope to budge.

I dove toward the the baseboard, looking for a crack. A tiny crevice. Anything. There had to be a way out.

Pssssssssssssssssss.

My fly hairs quivered in panic. The Controllers were shooting bug spray in through one of the bullet holes.

The bullet holes. Yes!

I darted toward the highest hole, closest to the ceiling. Perfect fit. I zipped through.

Air. Fresh air.

"A fly!"

Thwack!

A giant pink hand slammed against the ceiling. "Missed!"

Just barely, buddy. I shot sideways and down, close to the windows. They'd have to lean over the seats to reach me.

Thwack! Whack! Wham!

Hands, barf bags, rolled-up magazines, somebody's deliciously smelly sneaker. I dodged and darted, buzzing toward the door. Feeling fresh air blowing toward me.

Psssssssssss. Pssst-pssst-pssssssssssss.

Bug spray! Thick. Sticky. Toxic.

Fresh air. Follow the fresh air!

Psssssssssssssssssssss.

The spray clung to my legs, my body, my antennae. Every hair on my body was coated. My wings! I couldn't move my wings!

Daylight. I was out.

And falling. Like a missile. Then a rumble — a baggage cart? — and a gust of wind. It swept me sideways. I tumbled. Dropped. Tried to right myself, but couldn't tell which way was up. The world was a fog of darkness.

Whap.

I hit something and slid down.

"Where'd it go? I saw it fall."

Voices. Footsteps. Echoing through the fog.

Bigger. I had to get bigger or the bug spray

would kill me. I focused my mind on my human form. I could feel my body beginning to swell. My mind emerged from the fog.

I was in the baggage cart. The thing I'd hit was one of the few suitcases that hadn't flown out during my wild chase through the airport.

Footsteps shuffled past the cart.

Had to get out of there. I couldn't completely demorph to human. I'd be too big. I couldn't morph back to fly. There was enough bug spray clinging to my body to kill me.

I waited till the footsteps passed, then rolled out the other side and stumbled toward the next gate, too heavy to fly, too groggy to coordinate all six legs into a decent trot. Once again, a disgusting mutant creature straight out of the late, late show. I collapsed next to a conveyor belt.

"It has to be here. Spread out. FIND IT!"

I pulled myself onto the conveyor belt and burrowed under a golf bag. The belt rolled upward. The golf bag and I rolled with it. Then a lurch, and the golf bag flew through the air. I clung to the bottom with my sticky fly legs.

<Unnnnph.>

I landed on my back. The golf bag landed on top.

Thump. Thump. More suitcases. Crushing me in the darkness.

I had to demorph. Had to get out. I tried to

form a mental picture of myself. My human self. Cassie. But I was a jumble of wings, claws, skin, bulging eyes.

Skin. I focused on the skin. Human skin. Smooth. Swirling. Fading.

Fading to black.

CHAPTER 6

"Uhhhnn."

Frozen. Stiff. A frozen, stiff, throbbing ache. I swallowed. My throat was stuck shut.

I lay on my back — at least, I thought I was on my back — on the corner of something very hard. Something else, something heavy, was crushing my chest. And something steely and cold jabbed my cheek. My legs . . . did I even have legs?

All I could hear was a dull, relentless droning. My brain throbbed in time with the noise.

What was that noise, anyway?

I pushed the cold, hard thing away from my face. Curved. Metal. Felt like a golf club.

A golf club?

Oh. No.

It came back to me in a blur of bullets, bug spray, and a mental picture of my last known form. Basketball-sized half human with an extra pair of legs, stiff black hairs spiking out all over my body, and antennae.

How long had I been out? How long did it take to get this cold? It had to be more than two hours.

What if I was a mutant fly-girl *nothlit*?

"I can't even look," I moaned.

Moaned? My voice! My. Voice. My human voice.

I pushed against the golf bag. More suitcases tumbled down on top of me. I dug my way out. The light in the cargo hold was dim, but I could see my own body. Two legs, both ending in feet. Two arms. Two hands. Regulation, human-issue skin.

I touched my back. No wings. My head. No antennae.

I fell back against the frozen pile of luggage. "Thank God. Thank you, thank you, God."

Except —

I was in the cargo hold of a plane, nearly frozen, dying of thirst, and starving. MAN was I starving, jetting off to . . . where?

I checked the tag on the golf bag: SYD. Grabbed the suitcase next to it: SYD. Rummaged through the pile of bags. SYD. SYD. They all said SYD.

"SYD? What does that stand for?" I mumbled. "South Something Dakota?"

And how long would it take to get there? I rubbed my bare feet together. We could only morph skintight clothes, so all I was wearing was a flimsy black leotard. I blew on my hands. My breath came out in solid white puffs.

How many things could go wrong in one mission? It was only supposed to be a little surveillance at the airport. A bit of insurance.

Ax and Marco had found something interesting with their new Web-watch program. Information about a piece of alien spacecraft that had washed up on the beach a few hundred miles up the coast. A piece that sounded very much like part of a Yeerk ship. A Bug fighter.

Okay, so most of that Internet alien stuff is posted by paranoid nutcases. But like Marco said, you never know when a paranoid nutcase might be telling the truth. I mean, if I posted something about our little adventure at the airport, what would I sound like?

Besides, Marco and Ax found this piece of information on a closed Defense Department site in an encrypted, top-secret memo to the Joint

Chiefs of Staff. It takes way more than a security clearance and a secret code to defeat Ax.

The chunk of wreckage was being flown down in a commercial airliner, then transported to a Marine base, loaded onto a stealth jet, and flown to a NASA lab in Washington.

It was just what we were waiting for, proof that the Yeerks were here. On Earth. In America. If the government knew about the Yeerks, we wouldn't have to fight alone. The secret Yeerk invasion would no longer be a secret.

But if we knew about the chunk of Bug fighter, you could bet the Yeerks knew about it, too. They wouldn't want the wreckage tested. They wouldn't want NASA scientists to discover it was made from a metal not found on this planet. And they sure wouldn't want the media to spread the story.

Because the Yeerks don't want all-out war. They want to slowly, gradually infiltrate the human race so that by the time anybody notices what's been happening, it will be too late. Visser Three will have already won.

We were pretty sure they'd show up at the airport. And the Chee confirmed the story. The Chee couldn't get all the details, but they knew top-level Controllers in The Sharing had been in closed-door meetings, going over flight plans and airport blueprints.

They were all worked up — we were all worked up — over a hunk of metal. We could've been killed. We could've been captured.

And the two Marines. They could be dead. Or worse. Because of me. Because of my stupidity. Because I wanted to save a hunk of metal.

Which I hadn't saved anyway.

I pushed all the hard bags away and made a little nest of soft-sided suitcases. The cargo hold was full of huge metal crates marked "Boeing — Turbine PW400." My pile of luggage was sandwiched in between two of them.

I found two garment bags and wrapped one around my legs and the other around my shoulders. I wanted to unzip the bags and put on whatever was inside, preferably a parka. I wanted to rip open all the luggage and find something to eat.

But I couldn't. I was already a stowaway. I didn't want to be a thief, too.

Right. I could almost hear Marco's voice: *Let's see, Cassie, you pooped on a Controller, tossed two Marines into gun battle with evil aliens, probably got them and the armored truck guys captured or killed, and hijacked a baggage cart. Now you're worried about swiping snack crackers?*

I sniffed. Through the dust and must of the baggage I could smell oranges. Sweet, tangy.

I leaned out into the cargo hold. The orange smell grew stronger. On the other side of the metal crate I spotted a stack of boxes strapped to a pallet. They were all the same size and they were all marked ORANGES — NAVEL.

So many boxes. So many oranges. Would anyone really notice if one were missing?

I burrowed deeper into the stack of luggage and tried to ignore my hunger. And thirst. And the icy burning in my lungs every time I took a breath.

I needed to think. The plane would stop. Eventually. I'd just get off and find a phone.

Yeah, no problem. Just wait for somebody to open the cargo door, sashay down the conveyor belt, call my parents, and tell them to pick me up in South Dakota. Or South Yemen Desert. Or wherever the heck I ended up.

I sank back between the two crates. Why did everything have to be so difficult? Why couldn't I spend one single day worrying about something normal, like embarrassing teenage acne or the pop quiz I probably failed in algebra?

Well, the getting out wouldn't be so hard. I could morph a bird and fly out. Osprey this time, stronger and faster than a seagull. And then I could figure out where I was and how to get home.

Okay. That was the plan. I started to feel a little better. Morphing would solve the getting-out-of-the-airplane problem. Not the hunger. Or the thirst. Or the fingers and toes that were already turning slightly blue.

Except — wait a minute — yes, it could. I had the perfect cold-weather morph. Of course!

I felt warmer already. My head even quit throbbing.

And then I realized why.

The droning had stopped. The engines were silent. I waited for the plane to plummet toward Earth.

But it didn't. It was perfectly still. Motionless. Then —

ZZZZzzzzzzzzzttttttttt!

CHAPTER 7

Z ZZZzzzzzzzzttttttttt.

A blinding green light flashed through the cargo hold!

For a split second I could see the plane's steel bones through its metal skin. The green light penetrated suitcases and bags. Metal crates were suddenly transparent, showing huge engine parts inside.

Then the flash was gone. Black spots danced over my eyeballs.

I blinked. What was it?

But I knew: Yeerks. Somehow they'd figured out I was on board.

And I knew they weren't finished. They wouldn't X-ray the plane, then just go away.

I pushed the luggage and tried to stand. "Whoooaaaa."

I thumped sideways into one of the crates. My legs were dead. Not just stiff from the cold. Completely lifeless from the knees down.

The green light. But why did it only affect my legs?

I leaned against the crate.

The crate. Of course. My legs had been sticking out into the open cargo hold, but the rest of my body had been shielded by the engine parts inside the crate. Pure dumb luck had saved me.

So far.

I dragged myself back into my nest of luggage. Above me the passengers and crew were probably frozen in place. They didn't have huge turbofans protecting them from the green light. But they'd be okay. The Yeerks weren't interested in them. They'd thaw out, never knowing time had elapsed, never knowing they'd been paralyzed and unconscious.

Never knowing aliens had seized the plane in midflight.

Whhooosh!

The cargo door slid up. I peered around the edge of the crate.

A Bug fighter, hovering outside, holding the plane in place with some kind of tractor beam. The repulsive form of the Taxxon pilot filled the

Bug fighter's windows. An enormous centipede with a row of knife-edged teeth rimming the round mouth on top of its head. Its four globby eyes jiggled like red Jell-O.

My first instinct was to morph small. Hide.

"And be killed by a can of Raid? I don't think so." Rachel's words. If Rachel were here, that's exactly what she'd be saying. "They're ready for small. They're expecting you to run and hide. Don't give them what they want, Cassie."

The port of the Bug fighter rippled open. Two seven-foot aliens stood poised to leap into the plane's cargo hold. They glanced down at the miles of empty space between them and the plane, then turned and gestured toward the Taxxon.

They were Hork-Bajir, storm troopers of the Yeerk army. Feet of a T-rex. Blades of a room-sized Veg-O-Matic. Deadly blades that covered their elbows, wrists, knees, tails, and raked forward like daggers from their serpent heads.

They were armed with bug spray.

Okay, Rachel. So small wasn't the answer.

I had to think fast. What would Jake do? He'd . . . Well, he wouldn't have gotten himself stuck in this cargo hold in the first place. Neither would Tobias nor Ax. Or even Marco. They were too smart. Too careful.

And Rachel? Smart, yes. Careful, never. This

43

was exactly the kind of suicidal mess Rachel loved. And I knew what she'd be saying: "Surprise them. Morph something big. Fight back."

Win. Right. Against how many?

Two. This time Ax's voice echoed in my head.

Voices in my head. Definite sign of mental illness. Those golf clubs must have hit me harder than I thought.

But the voice made sense. A Bug fighter isn't that big. Cramming those two Hork-Bajir in there with the Taxxon pilot was already pushing it. No way anything else would fit. Get rid of them, and I'd be safe.

For a while.

The Taxxon was angling the Bug fighter closer to the cargo hold. The Hork-Bajir waited, bug spray in claw.

"Okay, Rachel," I whispered. "I'll fight to win."

I edged back between the crates and concentrated on the most powerful morph I possessed.

My shoulders bulged, up and out, joining the hulking muscles of my body. I felt my legs growing stronger, longer, thicker. Felt. Yes. The new DNA threw off the paralyzing effects of the green light.

Cuuuuuurrrrrrrruuuuuuunnnch.

Bones cracked and re-formed as my knees reversed, bending forward now instead of backward. My hands and feet thickened into paws the size of catchers' mitts. Claws shot from each toe.

The lower half of my face pushed out into a snout, tipped by a leather plug of a nose. My ears slid upward on my bulging skull. My human hair stiffened, hollowed, lightened to transparency, and spread to cover my body with fur.

My massive body. I was huge. Powerful. Unafraid. I hunkered down in the dim light between the two crates.

Ka-lunk.

The first Hork-Bajir leaped into the cargo hold. He peered through the darkness, then motioned toward the Bug fighter.

Ka-lunk.

The second Hork-Bajir jumped on board.

I could smell their musky stench, hear their talons clicking against the metal floor. My nose quivered. My ears twitched.

"GRRRAAAAAAAAAAWWWWRRRRR."

I reared up from the crates. The Hork-Bajir froze.

I didn't blame them. I was a bear. A polar bear. One of the most deadly creatures on Earth, when it wanted to be. I'd seen a polar bear sunbathe. I'd also seen a polar bear kick a grizzly bear's butt.

"GRRRAAAAAAAAAAWWWWRRRRR."

I lowered my girth against one of the metal

crates and gave it a shove. It skidded toward the Hork-Bajir.

"*HURR GAFRASCH!*" They dropped their spray cans and turned toward the Bug fighter.

Not in time.

Thunk.

The crate rammed into the Hork-Bajir, knocking them backward like a pair of bowling pins. They tumbled out into space, followed by the crate of engine parts.

"AAAAAAAAAhhhhhhhhhhhhh. . . ."

Their cries spiraled into silence.

I turned toward the Taxxon. Its Jell-O eyes bobbed.

Its claws tore at the Bug fighter's instrument panel.

Pffffffffffmmmmpp.

Another flash of light, orange this time. The airplane's engines roared to life. The Bug fighter veered away and down.

WWWHHHHHHHOOOOOOOOOSSSSHH.

Suction knocked me to the floor! The Bug fighter's tractor beam must have been pressurized, and now the pressure was gone. My fur felt like it was being ripped from my skin. Bags flew across the cargo hold, slammed into the wall, and shot into space. Cords ripped loose. Oranges smashed against the wall. The huge crates of airplane parts skidded toward the opening.

I lunged for a cargo net. It ripped loose from its metal brackets and whipped out into the clouds. I grabbed at the wall, the floor, something, anything! My claws scraped against metal.

Thuuuuud.

I slammed into a crate. And clung to it as it slid toward the open door.

CHAPTER 8

Crrrrreeeeeeeennnnnnnkkk.

Metal against metal. The crate skidded across the floor of the cargo hold. A suitcase burst open as it flew past me. Shirts and underwear flapped out into space.

I had to get the door closed! I dug my claws into the corners of the crate and reached one paw toward the ceiling. The suction nearly ripped off my front leg. I braced myself. The edge of the door was almost in reach. Another inch.

Crrrrreeeeeeeennnnnnnkkk.

The crate skidded forward. My paw brushed the edge of the door. I leaned and stretched.

Clannnnnngggkk.

<Ahhhhhh.>

The golf bag shot past, pummeling me with clubs. I felt the door slipping from my grasp. I dug my claws in and pushed. The door started to slide. Then —

The crate spun. I spun. Toward the opening! My front leg twisted, pulled. I could feel — could hear — tendons and muscles ripping. My claws broke free and scraped along the door.

<Nooooooooooo.>

My paw hit something solid. The door handle. I dug in and pulled with every muscle in my body.

The door slid forward and down.

Shhhhoooonk.

It latched shut. The whirlwind of luggage stopped. Boxes and suitcases dropped to the floor.

I collapsed against the wall of the cargo hold. Pain burned through my shoulder, numbing my front leg.

But I was okay. Okay.

Yeah. For now. But I knew the Taxxon pilot didn't leave because he was scared. He left to get reinforcements. The Yeerks would be back.

Back and ready to party. Oh, brother. Now Marco was in my head. Telling bad jokes.

I rolled to my feet. I needed to be ready. My bear body lumbered to the center of the plane, limping on three good legs. I surveyed the cargo hold: big, roomier now that half the luggage was

49

flying through the clouds. A total wreck now that the other half was strewn all over the floor.

There had to be something here I could use, something besides my remarkable talent for making a bad situation worse.

I plodded through a heap of mashed oranges. That heap could've been me, a big mound of mashed bear that had crashed to Earth. I shuddered. My fur rippled. Pulverized polar bear.

I stared at the oranges.

I rolled back on my haunches and licked the juice from my paws. They'd check, of course. They'd send more Bug fighters and more Controllers. They'd rip through the cargo hold from one end to the other, dousing every inch with pesticide.

But what if they didn't find me? Wouldn't they assume I'd been sucked through the door? That I'd joined the golf clubs in a mangled mess below?

Sorry, Rachel, but big wasn't the only way to fight back. As long as I was shielded from the green light, and big enough to survive the bug spray, all I had to do was hide.

I raised up on my hind legs and pawed along the ceiling. Nothing. Plodded around the cargo hold, checking the walls and the floor, from back to front. Nothing but sheet metal and rivets.

And then I saw it, at the front of the hold, half hidden behind a crate. My big weapon against alien invaders. A zipper. A thick canvas panel was set into the wall, and along the edge ran a big, heavy-duty zipper. I jabbed a claw into it and tugged. Presto. An opening.

I nosed the canvas aside.

It was some kind of control room. Lights, switches, and computerized gadgets lined the walls. I pushed my polar bear bulk inside. The room was about my size. I swung around. On the far wall was a ladder.

And at the top of the ladder, set into the ceiling, was a hatch with a lever in the center.

I reared up and pulled the lever. It turned. I nudged the hatch with one paw. It inched up. Light streamed through the crack around it. I could hear the sound of voices and clinking cups. Passengers.

I settled the hatch back into place, left it un-latched, and plodded back into the cargo hold.

My plan was taking shape, but none of it would work if I ended up frozen by the green beam. I picked four engine crates and shoved them, one by one, toward the canvas, heaving them into a circle next to the zippered opening.

Then I crouched beside the cargo door and scraped my claws along the floor, digging deep

51

gouges in the metal. I clawed similar gouges in the door itself, from the handle to the bottom edge. I sat back and admired my work. It definitely looked like the bear had been sucked from the plane while pulling down the door.

Good. I was ready.

I wanted to stay in morph. The bear was calm. Fearless. And warm. Almost too warm. But polar bear was too big for what I had planned.

I concentrated on my human form. Bones and muscles crunched and sloshed as the bear's bulk began shrinking, rearranging. Paws became hands and feet. Fur faded into skin. The pain in my shoulder shriveled to a pinprick, then vanished.

I was Cassie. Regular human Cassie, sitting on the cold metal floor of the cargo hold, about to pass out from hunger. Well, from hunger, fright, and exhaustion. But food would definitely help. And warmer clothes. My morphing outfit just wasn't cutting it.

I glanced around. I'd already lost most of the luggage. What was left lay in shreds around me. I threw off my guilt and began rummaging through suitcases.

Shorts. Tank tops. Bikinis. Oh, yeah, this stuff would keep me warm. Where were all the parkas?

I pried open an ancient square-cornered suitcase. Inside was a sweater. A man's cardigan. The elbows were threadbare, and the whole thing reeked of mothballs, but it was a sweater. Packed under two bottles of prune juice. Ick.

I rolled the bottles aside. The juice sloshed, wet and cold. I was thirsty. Too thirsty to be choosy. I picked up the juice bottles and put them in a little pile with the sweater. I felt kind of bad. Somewhere on this plane was an old man who'd probably end up cold and constipated before long.

But thirst was stronger than guilt.

I closed the suitcase and continued my search, gathering more clothes and what little food I could find. I unzipped a sports bag, and a cell phone fell out. My heart leaped. I flipped the phone open and punched ON. Nothing. SEND, END, CLEAR, OPERATOR. Still nothing. Not even static. I tossed it back into the bag.

I uncovered a hiking pack, the kind Boy Scouts use, with a sleeping bag strapped to the bottom. I untied the bag and dragged it into the space between the circle of crates with the rest of my loot.

I rolled the sleeping bag out on the floor of my little fort, put on my Mr. Rogers cardigan, and laid out my feast: prune juice, half a roll of breath mints, and an entire unopened box of Slim-Fast bars.

I slid into the sleeping bag and fluffed a bathrobe into a pillow. It was almost cozy. Almost like camp.

Space camp. Complete with evil aliens who were probably rocketing back toward the plane, preparing to attack.

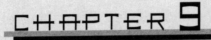

CHAPTER 9

ZZZZzzzzzzzzzttttttttt.

The green flash! I bolted upright. The engines were quiet. The plane had stopped.

Tsssssseeeeewwww. Ssssssssssssss.

I sniffed. Bug spray! The Yeerks were shooting some kind of pesticide missile into the cargo hold.

The smell was getting stronger. I threw off the sleeping bag. Prayed I had enough time.

Tsssssseeeeewwww. Ssssssssssssss.

I scrambled over the crates and through the opening in the canvas. Zipped it shut and swung up the ladder.

Ka-lunk.

I heard the first Hork-Bajir leap in the cargo hold. Its tyrannosaur claws clicked across the metal.

Ka-lunk.

A second Hork-Bajir. Then —

Thump.

Another sound. Softer. Something else had landed in the cargo hold, something besides a Hork-Bajir.

I'd reached the top of the ladder. I pushed on the ceiling hatch. It didn't budge! I jerked the lever. It was unlatched, but it wouldn't open.

A voice, a woman's voice, coming from the cargo hold: "The Andalite could still be on board. Search every inch!"

A human-Controller. That softer sound had been a human-Controller leaping onto the plane.

I pushed on the hatch again, quietly, firmly. It inched up. I could see a sliver of light. But the panel was heavy. Something was on top of it, holding it down.

The woman's voice again: "We're showing a slight movement on the sensors. Keep searching."

Sensors?

I glanced around. The control room was wide

open. No place to hide. I had to get up into the cabin! Get up, hide, and stop moving. I hooked my elbow around the top rung of the ladder, braced my feet, and gave the hatch a shove, using my legs for leverage.

The panel inched up. I wedged my shoulder against it and pushed. Another inch. Up. More light. Then it broke free. I lunged through the hole. The panel fell to the side with a thud.

CLANGGGKK-CRUNNNNCH.

A crash of dishes and metal.

"The Andalite!"

I bolted up through the opening. I was in an aisle, directly under the feet of a flight attendant who'd been paralyzed while serving coffee. Her beverage cart must have been parked on top of the hatch. It had crashed into a passenger and was now tipped sideways, two wheels still spinning in the air.

"Upward movement! The sensors show upward movement. To the front of the hold. NOW!"

I leaped to my feet.

"GO!"

"*ANDALITE HAUT!*"

I could hear the Hork-Bajir below, ripping through the canvas. They were too big to fit through the opening, but they were armed.

Tssssseeeeeeewwwww! Tssssseeeeeeewwwww!

57

Dracon beams seared through the hatch.

I grabbed a pot from the flight attendant's hand and poured still-scalding coffee down the hole.

"AHHHHHHH!"

I raced down the aisle.

Tssssssseeeeeeewwwww!

A Dracon beam exploded into the cabin behind me.

I had to hide. And stay still. Any movement would give me away. I could morph something small — squirrel, skunk, bat — but I had to find a place to hide! Where?

Not the bathroom. They'd definitely check this time. Not the baggage compartments or the cockpit. There had to be someplace! I whirled. A plane full of passengers stared at me with unmoving eyes.

The passengers. Yes! I could pretend to be one of the frozen passengers. Hide in plain sight.

I dove toward an empty seat.

Oh, yeah, that'd work. A barefoot girl in a leotard and a cardigan. Blended right in.

Tsssseeeeeeewwwww! Tsssseeeeeeewwwww!

Dracon beams blasted through the floor, widening the opening.

Cccccrrrreeeeeeeeeeaaaaaaankkkk.

58

Metal ripped.

I grabbed an airplane blanket off the guy in the next row and threw it over my body.

Tsssssssseeeeeeewwwww!

A Hork-Bajir burst into the cabin.

CHAPTER 10

A second Hork-Bajir followed, and then a woman, the human-Controller, in running shoes and a warm-up suit.

"The movement has stopped."

She looked like a gym teacher. A gym teacher carrying a big-game rifle under one arm. In her other hand she held something that looked like a Game Boy.

I kept my eyes forward, unblinking.

The gym teacher studied the gadget in her hand. "Not even a blip. Our clever Andalite is hiding." She swung around to face the Hork-Bajir. "FIND IT."

The jetliner had two aisles and three banks of seats. The Hork-Bajir each took an aisle. Started to rip open baggage compartments, fire Dracon beams under the seats.

"Stop shooting, you idiots!" The gym teacher swung her rifle toward the Hork-Bajir. "You'll kill us all! Besides, our orders are to bring the Andalite back alive. Damaged, perhaps. But still breathing. If it dies" — she cocked the rifle — "you die."

I tensed. I couldn't let them find me. No matter what happened, they couldn't take me alive. Tobias had been captured, and I knew some of the horror he'd faced. The physical torture, the mind games, the hallucinations.

He didn't talk about it much. Tobias was strong. Tough. Hardened by his time as a hawk.

But they'd almost broken him.

If the Yeerks could do that to Tobias, what chance would I have? How could I keep our secrets? If they captured me, my friends would be toast. Sure, in some weird way maybe I'm the biggest risk taker, bigger even than Rachel. But torture?

I fixed my eyes on the seat in front of me. Was aware of the Hork-Bajir ripping down the aisle again. Ransacking overhead bins and shoving frozen legs aside to search under the seats. I counted the rows between him and me: four.

Three.

Two.

61

Didn't breathe.

The Hork-Bajir shoved his Dracon beam under the seat in front of me and swung it from side to side. He pulled out a woman's purse and two carry-on bags. Dumped them in the aisle.

"NOTHING."

I nearly choked on my own spit.

Seven feet of bladed nightmare towered above me, so close I could feel the warmth of his skin, his rank breath puffing down on my face.

My skin prickled. Goose bumps. I prayed the Hork-Bajir didn't see.

Slaaamm!

He threw open the luggage compartment over my head. Tore through the bags, then bent down to check under my seat. He gave my legs a shove. I toppled over onto the chunky guy next to me. My blanket started to slide. One bare foot slipped out.

The Hork-Bajir didn't notice.

He tossed the carry-on bags into the aisle. Snorted and straightened to his full height. His elbow blade sliced past, an inch from my ear. Then he turned to the row behind me.

The breath I'd been holding slid from my lungs.

But I couldn't relax, not even a little. The human-Controller still stood at the front of the cabin, watching, waiting.

My eyeballs burned. I needed to blink.

I heard a door bang behind me. A toilet lid slammed.

"Andalite not here."

"Fine. We'll check up front." The human-Controller glanced once more at the passengers, then turned toward the cockpit door.

The Hork-Bajir charged past me up the aisle.

I allowed myself to breathe. And swallow. Once they entered the cockpit, I would escape. Somehow.

The human-Controller slid the door open and started to step through. Then she stopped and turned, slowly, her eyes narrowed.

I froze.

"The Andalite bandit could be under our very noses." She gazed from passenger to passenger. "Set your beams on low and see if anybody jumps. Remember — capture, don't kill."

She stepped into the cockpit. The two Hork-Bajir adjusted their Dracon beams then each started down an aisle.

Tsseew.

The Hork-Bajir in my aisle zapped a business-man in the front row. The businessman didn't move.

Tsseew.

The woman next to him.

No reaction.

The Hork-Bajir worked his way toward the back of the plane, blasting each passenger's arm.

Tsseew! Tsseew!

The stench of charred flesh burned my nostrils.

The passengers sat motionless. They couldn't feel the jolt. The burn. The pain that knifed through their bodies.

But I would.

I'd been blasted by Dracon beams before. I would feel the pain, and I would react. No matter how hard I tried, how much I steeled myself, I would react.

I could keep myself from screaming. Maybe. But the slightest flinch would give me away. A blink, a jerk, even a quick breath.

The Hork-Bajir moved toward me, passenger by passenger, row by row.

I was trapped.

CHAPTER 11

I swallowed my panic and tried to think. It was too late to morph. The Hork-Bajir would see the movement. He'd be on me in one leap.

I watched.

The Hork-Bajir in the other aisle worked fast. He was about three rows ahead of my Hork-Bajir. I could see him out of the corner of my eye, working on the aisle directly across from me. He fired, watched for a reaction, then moved on. He was behind me now, out of view.

The Hork-Bajir in my aisle moved closer. Leaned over the row in front of me and fired.

Tsseew!

He watched.

Tsseew!

65

He waited.

Tsseew!

Nothing.

He turned to my row.

I froze. I had a chance. One chance. But I had to time my moves perfectly.

The Hork-Bajir leaned over me. His elbow blade whipped past my face. He aimed his Dracon beam at the guy next to the window.

I raised my hand behind him, slowly, steadily, holding my eyes straight ahead, the rest of my body motionless.

Tsseew!

As the Hork-Bajir fired, I pushed my hand against his back.

He jerked at the touch, then slumped forward, as lifeless as the passengers around us.

I was acquiring him, absorbing his DNA, and he had fallen into the acquiring trance. He wouldn't stay that way long, but if I were quick and quiet, it might be long enough for me to escape.

The Hork-Bajir swayed. I saw his hand relax, saw the Dracon beam balanced on his fingertips. I reached for it.

Too late!

The Dracon clattered to the floor.

"ANDALITE!" the other Hork-Bajir shouted.

I dove.

TSEEEEEEEEEWWWWWWWW!

The Hork-Bajir above me exploded into nothing.

I inched backward on my belly.

TSEEEEEEEEEWWWWWWWW!

The blast incinerated the seat beside me.

I'd landed on the other Dracon beam, and now I grabbed it.

Ka-lump.

The Hork-Bajir leaped over the frozen passengers in the middle seats. His claws dug into the carpet less than a foot from my face.

I aimed.

TSEEEEEEEEEWWWWWWWW!

The Hork-Bajir vaporized in a cloud of black smoke.

I stared at the Dracon beam in horror. I'd only meant to stun him! The weapon must have knocked to full power when it hit the floor.

I leaped to my feet. Not the time. Had to get away! I raced toward the front of the plane, side-swiping the overturned coffee cart and hurdling the hole in the floor. I couldn't go back down through the hatch. I'd be trapped. The Bug fighter pilot would see me trying to escape through the cargo door.

There was only one way out, and I had to reach it before —

"What's going on out here?" The human-

67

Controller stepped from the cockpit. "Did you find the —"

I stopped dead.

She stopped dead.

I glanced toward the passenger door. It was halfway between us.

"How very clever." The Controller raised her rifle. "Morphing a child to throw off suspicion." She aimed. "It almost worked."

I was still holding the Dracon beam. It would get me out the door. Easy. I gripped the handle and slid my finger onto the trigger.

But it was on full power. One blast would eliminate her from the planet.

I couldn't pull the trigger.

I had to distract her.

"You can't shoot me," I said.

"Oh?" she laughed. "Watch me."

I swallowed. "Okay, maybe you're right. Visser Three wanted the Andalite bandit taken alive, but if you explain to him how a simple airplane search spun out of control, forcing you to kill me, I'm sure he'd understand." I shot a glance at the door handle, then at the rifle leveled at my head. "He's an extremely nice person."

The human-Controller hesitated.

It was all I needed. I lunged, wrenched the

door handle, and pushed. It swung open easily. No suction. The tractor beams were keeping the plane pressurized.

Still clutching the Dracon beam, I dove into space.

CHAPTER 12

"Aaaaaaaahhhhhh!"

Flying is incredible. Riding the thermals, feeling the lift beneath your wings, soaring through the endless blue of the sky.

"Aaaaaaaahhhhhh!"

Falling headfirst from two miles up, with no wings and nothing resembling a parachute — not as fun.

Two Bug fighters hovered on either side of the plane, their pressurizing beams trained directly on the fuselage. I dove straight down between them.

One Bug fighter faced away from me. The other was partially hidden from view by the plane. The pilots didn't see me blow past.

Wind pummeled my face and drove the Dracon beam into my chest. I gripped the weapon in one hand and held my arms and legs out, spread-eagle style, to slow the dive. My cardigan billowed out above me.

I had to morph! Something fast. With wings. Osprey.

I concentrated on the bird's form. Caught a movement out of the corner of my eye. Using my hands and feet as rudders, I angled around for a better view.

It was a Bug fighter, the one that had been hovering outside the cargo door. It pulled away from the plane, swung around, and dove. The Taxxon pilot's hideous body bulged against the windshield as the spacecraft bore down on me.

I judged the distance between him and me and between me and the solid earth that was rushing up toward us. I could finish the morph and dive, maybe losing him near the ground.

But he'd see me. He'd see me morph directly to osprey, and he'd know I was human.

That little news flash would probably get him promoted to Visser Four.

And get my friends sentenced to death.

I shuddered. Those were my choices: Die. Or kill my friends.

Or —

There was another way to eliminate the prob-

71

lem. I slid my finger onto the Dracon beam's trigger. And that was to . . . eliminate the problem. I pulled my hands together above my head, gripped the weapon, and aimed.

TSEEEEEEEEEEEEEEEEEEW!

The windshield shattered. The Taxxon burst like a melon, spewing its guts across the sky. The Bug fighter spiraled out of control, a flaming missile spinning toward Earth.

Ka-PLOOOOOOOOOOOOOOOSH.

It exploded. The blast ripped the Dracon beam from my fingers and knocked me upward and back in a shower of glass and metal.

I was spinning now, end over end. Sky. Clouds. Earth. Clouds fading away. Earth looming larger. Had to get control! Fast.

I closed my eyes and focused. Wings, talons, feathers. But mostly wings. Please give me wings.

Bones popped and crunched. My shoulders wrenched back. Legs jerked forward.

Splooot! My nose and mouth shot out, the skin hardening into a beak.

I felt the cardigan puff up around me. I flapped to be free of it.

Flapped. Yes! I opened my eyes. The cardigan whipped from my shrinking body. I had wings. Or the beginnings of wings. A pattern of lines appeared on my skin, like a tattoo that swept across my body then burst into full-fledged feathers. Osprey feathers.

My wings lifted. I rose on a pocket of warm air only a few feet above the sparse brush below. Floated for a moment to gain my bearings, then spilled the air from my wings and swooped toward Earth.

The ground was red and barren and endless. I soared low over the scrub, looking for landmarks. A town. A road sign. Even a road. Something to give me clue where I was.

Pffffffffffmmmmpp.

An orange flash.

A wave of fear swept through my bird body.

Shuh-ROOOOOOMMMMMMMMMMMFF.

The sound of a jet, above and behind me.

I circled. The plane roared away from me across the sky. The single Bug fighter remained, hovering. My osprey eyes could see the gym teacher crammed in beside the Taxxon pilot. She waved her arms and pointed. Down. At me.

I whirled and shot along the ground, weaving in and out between scraggly bushes.

The shadow slid over me.

TSSSSSSSEEEEEEEW!

I wheeled. There had to be someplace to hide. Something in this barren desert that would shield me.

TSSSSSSSEEEEEEEW.

73

Red dirt exploded around me.

I swerved. I could feel the strength drain from my wings. My osprey body was built to glide and soar, and the endless pumping so close to the ground was wearing me down.

I skimmed low, over a clump of grass, under a bush, around a scrawny tree —

— and out into space.

I banked. It was a ravine, narrow and deep, a dry creek bed gouged into the flat red earth. I flew in close to the wall of the creek bed, darting along under an overhanging of rocks and scrub.

A shadow darkened the ravine, then disappeared.

TSSSSSSSEEEEEEEW!

An explosion, further up the creek bed.

I pushed my wings forward. Lowered my talons. Landed on a rocky outcrop.

The shadow passed again, slipping over me in the opposite direction.

TSSSSSSSEEEEEEEW!

A blast in the distance. They'd lost me.

The wall of the ravine was pitted with small hollows. I chose a deeper one and demorphed.

I crouched in the hollow and took a deep breath. Human again, but not for long. I could hear the Bug fighter blowing craters across the desert. But my mind focused on something else. I closed my tired eyes and concentrated.

Elbows and hips scraped against rocks as I shrank to a microscopic dot. My body flattened. Bones dissolved. An extra pair of legs sprouted from my armor-plated body. Piercing tubes shot from my mouth.

I was a wingless, bloodsucking parasite, blind and ravenous.

A flea.

I burrowed into the sand and waited.

CHAPTER 13

The ground trembled. Another Dracon blast. And another.

I couldn't hear them. Fleas don't have ears. But I sensed each tremor with every molecule of my body. Grains of sand the size of garbage trucks shifted around me.

But they couldn't hurt me. Unless the Yeerks fired directly on top of me, I was safe.

For two hours anyway.

I burrowed deeper into the sand. The flea's instincts weren't hard to control. Basically it has only two: Find blood. Eat. And once it figured out there wasn't any blood in this little sandpile, the flea brain was pretty quiet.

My own brain, however, was on overload.

I'd been running and running and fighting and running and mostly screwing things up since . . .

Since when? How long had it been since I'd casually drifted above the airport, watching for a top-secret shipment? Years, it seemed. Another lifetime. Somebody else's lifetime.

But it couldn't have been more than a few hours. Twelve maybe? Fourteen? Fourteen horrible hours?

Horrible. Right.

Horrible is getting to school and finding out you left your homework on the bus, your boyfriend is dumping you, and your socks don't match. This was beyond horrible. This was . . .

There wasn't even a word for it.

An image pushed itself into my head. Two Hork-Bajir, staring at me in helpless terror as they tumbled backward from the cargo hold. Their screams echoed through my brain.

They didn't deserve it. Yeah, Hork-Bajir look like death on two legs, but without a Yeerk in their heads, they're a simple species, innocent and trusting. And those blades? To a Hork-Bajir, a free Hork-Bajir, they serve one purpose: to strip bark from trees. For food. Hork-Bajir are vegetarians. Gentle, nature-loving vegetarians.

And I'd killed four of them in less than a day.

The two in the cabin of the plane had been an

accident. I hadn't actually pulled the trigger on the first one, and I'd only meant to stun the second. Still, if I hadn't been there, they'd be alive. And what about the two Hork-Bajir in the cargo hold? Not an accident. I had meant to kill them, and I did.

Just like I'd meant to kill the Taxxon.

I could almost hear Rachel: "Puh-leaze, Cassie. Taxxons are willing Controllers and pure cannibals. That pilot would've gobbled up his own splattered guts if he'd had a mouth left to do it with. Don't waste your sympathy. Or your guilt. Somebody had to die, you or him, and you chose him. End of story."

Yeah, the end of a story that shouldn't have started.

If I'd made even one good decision, one smart move, in the last twelve or fourteen or however many hours, none of this would have happened.

Bald Spot wouldn't have gone nuts. The Marines wouldn't have started shooting. I would have bailed when Jake gave orders to abort the mission. And I wouldn't have fallen unconscious in the cargo hold of a plane, left with no choice but to kill or be killed.

I'm not trying to be some kind of martyr, or say that I'm always a screwup. I'm not. In my world, making hard choices is part of the deal. Sometimes I'm right, sometimes I'm wrong. Sometimes I just can't tell, even when the mission is over and we've all come out alive, at least.

Leave the Animorphs. Come back. Trust Aftran, the Yeerk. Trust her again. Take responsibility for the never-ending, always unfolding consequences of those decisions. Say, no, I can't be part of this mission, can't be part of a mass killing of innocent people no matter what the ultimate goal, I won't. Get involved anyway, commit acts maybe much worse. Why? To save some lives, not others. A choice. There's always a choice.

And if I'd made other, smarter choices this time, I'd be home now, taking care of sick animals in my parents' barn.

Well, at least that was one thing I didn't have to worry about. My parents wouldn't know I was gone. The Chee would be covering for me, like they usually did.

Jake had probably alerted them as soon as he saw I was missing. Now one of the Chee was projecting a holographic image of me so real my own parents wouldn't notice the difference. The Chee was eating my meals, going to my classes, helping my dad with the animals.

Kissing my parents good night.

And also doing my algebra homework, so there was a tiny up side.

Meanwhile, I was a flea, hiding in the dirt. And I didn't even know where.

I had to get home.

I wanted my parents. I wanted my farm.

I missed Jake. And Rachel. Tobias and Ax. Even Marco.

The Chee couldn't cover for me forever. Could they?

My two hours were probably up. I demorphed. Slowly. Cautiously.

Night had fallen. Above me all I could see were stars and a full moon sitting low in the sky. No Bug fighters. No stalled-out airplanes. No gym teacher gunning for me with an elephant rifle.

I stood and peeked over the edge of the ravine. Nothing. A wide flat stretch of nothing.

"Okay." I brushed sand from my hair. "This is good. I don't know where I am, but apparently the Yeerks don't, either. Definite improvement. I can work with this." I stared across what looked like an endless desert. "I think."

I grabbed hold of a root and pulled myself from the ravine. I crouched low, half expecting an army of Hork-Bajir to appear out of the darkness.

That's when I heard the voice, right in my ear: "They're gone."

CHAPTER 14

"AAAHHH!"
"AAAHHH!"
"Gggrrrrrrrrrrrrrrrrr."
I screamed.
He screamed.
His dog flattened himself against the ground in front of his master and let out a low growl.

I crept backward in the dirt.

"It's okay, Tjala." The kid reached out to scratch the dog's neck. He glanced up at me, then lowered his eyes. "He won't bite you," he said.

The kid was about my age, maybe older. It was hard to tell in the moonlight. He'd been sitting between a big rock and a clump of bushes,

81

and I'd practically landed in his lap when I'd climbed out of the ravine. His skin was dark, darker than mine. He dissolved into the night shadows.

I glanced around. What else was lurking in the dark?

"No worries," he said. "We are alone."

I glanced around again, not sure whether or not to believe him. "Man," I said. "You scared me."

"I scared *you*?" He laughed. His dark curls bobbed. The dog's ears twitched. "That's funny."

"Yeah. Hysterical." I pulled myself out of the dirt and started to brush off my clothes. I peeked up at the kid and caught him staring at my leotard.

He looked quickly away.

I glanced down. Okay, so the thing was in shreds. Rachel would be thrilled. She'd get to take me shopping for a new one when I got home.

If I got home. I looked up. "Um —"

The kid smiled. "You'll be needing some help."

"Uh, yeah."

What was it with him? It was like he was reading my mind. His voice was soft, and a little shy, but also confident. Like he knew what needed to be done and was willing do it. Kind of like . . . Jake.

I shook my head. No, nothing like Jake.

"Yeah, I could use some help. I'm sort of —" Gee, how was I going to explain suddenly appearing out of nowhere? "Lost."

"Lost." He laughed again. "The bird-girl who can change into a bug is lost. No worries. Now you're found." He climbed to his feet. "I'm Yami and I'll be your guide for the evening." He smiled. "I like to say that. One of my uncles is a tour guide at Uluru."

Yami turned and loped off along the creek bank. Tjala the dog trotted behind him.

"I'm Cassie," I hollered after them. "And thanks. I think."

I ran to catch up before I lost them both in the dark. I stumbled about as I followed them through the scrub, trying to keep my bare feet on the soft sand and away from rocks and sticks and prickly clumps of grass.

Yami was barefoot, too, but his skinny legs rambled along with a natural grace. Tjala bounded along at his side. He was a sturdy little dog, not more than a half-grown pup, with dark speckles all over his coat and sharp ears that perked up at every rustle and birdcall.

We walked in silence for a few moments.

83

"So," I finally said. "You saw all that back there, huh? The bird? The flea?"

Yami nodded. "And the funny airplane." He shook his head. "Many planes fly over, but I've never seen one like that before, chasing birds and blowing holes in the ground. It was a surprise."

The Bug fighter. A surprise. Yeah, you could call it that.

I tripped over a scruffy bush. "But the bird changing to a girl, then to a flea, then back to a girl again? That wasn't a surprise?"

Yami gave me a little sideways smile. "No." He shrugged one shoulder. "Okay, maybe a little. But — "

He stopped suddenly and held his arm out at his side. I almost ran into it.

" — but not a lot. This is why."

He lowered his arm. I caught my breath. The flat desert floor had come to an abrupt end. We were standing at the edge of a crescent-shaped cliff.

Tjala's ears twitched.

"Grrrrrrrrrrrrrrr."

"Ssssh." Yami held his hand on Tjala's back to keep him still. "Stay."

The dry creek bed ended at the edge of the cliff. I peeked over. The full moon was reflected below. The cliff walls dropped straight down to a pool of water.

"It's a sacred place," said Yami. "A spring, created by our spirit ancestors. They made the water and the cliff and all the caves along the cliff. And when they finished, they changed themselves into rocks and mountains and trees and stars and all the things on Earth and in the sky." He gave me his one-shoulder shrug and flashed a grin. "And maybe fleas, too. Who knows?"

Tjala stood at the edge of the cliff dead still, every muscle tensed. His ears pitched forward.

"Grrrrrrrrrrrrr."

"No, Tjala. Stay." Yami scratched Tjala's head. He looked at me and motioned toward something below.

I followed his gaze. The moonlight fell on a herd of large animals grazing in the grass along the water's edge. Some were hunched over, eating. Some stood upright on their huge back legs, almost like humans, their long ears twitching. One of the smaller ones, a baby, turned and leaped into its mother's pouch.

"Okay," I said. "This is not South Dakota."

CHAPTER 15

"South Dakota?" Yami gave me a funny look. "You *are* lost."

No kidding. I gazed down at the herd of kangaroos. Lost in Australia. About as far away from home as I could get without leaving the planet.

But the kangaroos! I stared at them. They were such an odd combination of parts: the face of a deer, the ears of a rabbit, the long, long tail of a rat stretching out behind them on the ground.

When they bent over to eat, they were an awkward tangle of tail and legs, their big furry rumps higher than their heads. When they stood, they held their smaller front legs at their sides, like a human.

And somehow all the odd and curious parts came together in a magnificent whole.

"I didn't know they were so big," I whispered.

"These are reds," said Yami. "Taller than my grandfather. This mob grazes here often."

"Mob?"

Yami shrugged. "A bunch of 'roos. A mob."

I nodded. A mob. I couldn't take my eyes off them.

And neither could Tjala.

"Grrrrrrrrrrrrrr."

The kangaroos stopped grazing and looked up.

"Stay, Tjala."

Tjala turned his head toward Yami, then back toward the kangaroos. One of the bigger ones leaped. Its huge back feet thumped against the grass.

Tjala bounded along the edge of the cliff and scrambled down where the land began sloping toward the plain below.

"No!" Yami raced after him. I followed.

The kangaroos bolted. They didn't stampede like cattle. They hopped in all different directions, zigzagging across the grass, their hind feet thundering over the ground.

Tjala leaped onto the grassy plain and ran in circles around the 'roos, nipping at their legs. The kangaroos kicked and swiped at him with their claws.

Yami climbed down a gully that cut through the side of the steep hill. I followed, stumbling around boulders and tripping over gnarled roots.

The mob had scattered. Tjala was still chasing one of the big 'roos. It kicked at him, leaning back on its thick tail and raking Tjala's nose with its hind claws.

Tjala howled.

The kangaroo leaped into the water. Tjala splashed in after it.

"No!" Yami ran toward the spring. "Come back, Tjala!"

The pup splashed about in the shallow water near the shore. He looked at Yami, then back at the water, torn between obeying his master and chasing the kangaroo.

Yami slapped his knees. "Tjala! Come!"

Tjala gave the 'roo one last longing look, then turned and bounded toward Yami. He nearly wagged himself in half as Yami knelt down to scratch his neck.

The kangaroo swam to the far shore. It hopped a short distance away, then turned back to look at us. It watched us for a moment, then turned again and hopped off into the night.

"It seems okay," I said. "I don't think Tjala hurt it."

"I wasn't worried about the 'roo." Yami

laughed and fell over backward as Tjala leaped up to lick his face. "I was worried about Tjala. That big boomer would have killed him."

"Really?"

Yami patted Tjala's back. "I have seen a big boomer drown two dingoes this way. He led them into the deep water and held their heads under. Two wild dingoes at one time."

Yami climbed to his feet and started off across the grass. Tjala started to follow, then stopped. His ears perked up.

I listened. A rustling and thumping.

Yami listened, too, then nodded and loped off toward the sound. Tjala and I followed.

We found a female kangaroo — a doe, Yami called it — caught in a woven fence. One of her hind legs was pushed between the wires. She held her head up and back as she kicked and clawed. Her joey peeked out of her pouch. Ducked down inside when it saw us.

Yami held Tjala still while I crept up behind the kangaroo.

"Take great care," he said. "Keep far from her claws."

The kangaroo twisted and kicked. She whipped her head around. Her eyes held a wild, frantic look.

"Shhhhh," I said. "You're going to be okay."

I pressed my hand against her tail. She thrashed once more, then fell into the acquiring trance.

I had to work fast. One of her back claws was caught in the woven wire. Her kicking had wrapped several more wires around her leg. I stretched a strand of wire to untangle it.

The joey poked his nose out of the pouch and looked up at me.

"Hey, little guy," I said. "Your mama's going to be free in a second."

I pulled the last wire from her claw, then backed away.

The mother kangaroo lifted her head. Her ears twitched. She sniffed her joey, then rolled to her feet and bounded off.

Bummmph. Bummmph. Bummmph.

She stopped under a stand of knotted trees and turned. She stood upright, watching me. Her long ears flicked. Then she turned again and hopped away.

Yami smiled, his sideways smile. "You have a special way with kangaroos," he said. "Maybe the bird-girl wants to change into a 'roo next time instead of a flea?"

He laughed. I laughed, too. Yami thought turning into a kangaroo was a pretty funny joke.

I didn't tell him the joke was now entirely possible.

CHAPTER 16

"**H**AHAHAHA!"

A booming laugh burrowed into my dreams.

I opened my eyes, closed them, then opened them again. The sun blazed across a sea of red sand.

Red sand. Oh, yeah. Australia.

I could still hear the laugh, and the sound of voices. I lifted my head. I was lying on a hard wooden bench on Yami's porch. Someone had rolled up a blanket and slipped it under my head, and now my neck was molded around it. My shoulder was numb where it had been jutting into the wood.

It had to be morning, early morning, but the air was already so thick with heat I could barely

91

move through it. I swung my legs over the side of the bench and sat up.

I remembered following Yami to his family's outpost. No, not outpost. Outstation. That's what he'd called it, an outstation. I remembered waiting on the bench while Yami went to find his mother. I remembered resting my head on my arm when I leaned over to pet Tjala.

And that's all I remembered. Until now.

The talking and laughing were coming from outside. I wiped the sleep from my eyes and stood up. I had to find Yami and see if I could use his phone. I had to get home. Somehow.

At the very least, I had to get out of here. The Yeerks would be back, and I couldn't put Yami and his family in more danger than I already had.

Yami's house was a small stone rectangle, low to the ground, with a metal roof that extended out on all four sides to form a porch. Nearby I could see a couple of other houses and a little silver camper.

Yami was sitting with a bunch of other people, his family, I guessed, inside a lean-to made of branches. They fell silent when they saw me walking toward them across the sand.

Oh, no, had my leotard — ? I glanced down.

Thank goodness. It was filthy, torn, and sticky with sweat, but it still covered all the important parts.

Tjala bounded from the lean-to and raced toward me across the sand. He wagged and wiggled and licked my hand, then turned and ran back to the lean-to. I followed.

When I reached the lean-to, Yami gave me a quick half smile and motioned his head toward an old man sitting in the center. "My grandfather wants to meet you," he said.

The man unfolded his legs and stood up. He wore a sleeveless workshirt and dusty jeans. His hair was a tangle of gray curls, tamed slightly by a red headband, and his face looked like it had been carved from seasoned wood, with a broad, curving nose and a forehead that jutted out so far it hid his eyes completely.

He swayed. One leg almost buckled under him. Yami reached for his arm and held him till he regained his balance.

The old man studied me. The wind lifted his long, grizzled beard.

And then he smiled, a smile like Yami's that filled his entire face. He took my hand in his and clasped it softly. He nodded and laughed, a deep booming laugh. The laugh that had woken me up.

The rest of Yami's family laughed, too, and gathered around me.

I looked at Yami.

He shrugged. "I told my grandfather about

93

your great shape-shifting powers. And about how you calmed the 'roo. And about how you hid in a creek bed that runs into the spring."

Oh. That.

Yami's grandfather nodded. "The spring of our ancestors. You chose it as your safe shelter. It is a sign."

Yeah. It was a sign all right. A sign that I shouldn't be set loose in the world unsupervised.

But Yami's family didn't see it that way. Apparently I'd become something of a celebrity while I was sleeping.

Yami explained it to me. "My grandfather's greatest fear is that the old traditions will disappear. He works very hard to teach us the ways of our ancestors. He thinks you are proof that he is doing well."

I stared at him, horrified. "But Yami, I'm not. I'm not proof of anything."

Yami only shrugged.

His mother gave me a T-shirt and shorts and insisted I'd be cooler in them. She was right. I was a little cooler. But I panicked when I came back outside from changing clothes and saw Yami's aunts throwing my leotard in a tub to soak.

"I'll need to take that with me," I said. "Soon."

They nodded and fixed me breakfast, a big bowl of something that looked like miniature white Taxxons.

"Witchetty grub," said Yami.

"Ah." I stared into the bowl. It was filled with fat, white, segmented worms, longer than my hand. "Don't tell me," I said. "Tastes like chicken."

Yami frowned. "No." He popped a grub into his mouth and chewed. "More like butter. You try."

He picked the longest, plumpest grub from his bowl and held it out to me.

I stared at him, then at the grub. I'd eaten worse. Actually, I'd been worse, when I was in Yeerk morph. But right now I was Cassie, regular human Cassie, and there was no way I was biting into a wormy little Taxxon.

"You know, this desert heat is really getting to me." I swallowed. "I — I just don't have an appetite."

Yami blinked and nodded. His smile faded. I looked into his dark eyes, and a little pain stabbed through my heart.

We were by ourselves, sitting side by side in the little lean-to. Tjala dozed at Yami's side. His grandfather had hobbled off toward one of the houses, and his little cousins were playing in the

95

sand nearby. The rest of his family had finally stopped fussing over me and gone about their morning work.

Yami dropped the grub back into his bowl.

"Yami," I said, "your family has been so nice to me. You have been so nice to me."

I touched his arm. He looked down at it, surprised. I was a little surprised myself. I pulled my hand back.

"I don't want you to think I don't appreciate everything, and I know I sound like E.T., but I have to phone home. It's a long-distance call." A really long distance. "But I can reverse the charges. I think."

He gave me a sad smile. "We don't have a telephone."

I stared at him.

"You could use the two-way radio." He looked down at his bowl. "But the explosion yesterday destroyed the aerial."

"The explosion?" I frowned. "Oh, no."

The Bug fighter. When I Draconed the Bug fighter, I'd fried their radio antenna. I couldn't call out. Yami's family couldn't call out. Not only had I led the Yeerks to their outstation, I'd destroyed their only means of communication.

"Oh, Yami. I'm so, so sorry." I took a deep breath. "And I know I must seem like a total idiot to you, just falling from the sky and demanding

96

phone service. It's just that nobody knows where I am. I'm not even sure where I am."

"I know where you are." Now Yami touched my arm. "You're in the Piti Spring Community," he explained. "Northern Territory, Australia." He smiled. "Not South Dakota."

I laughed. "Thank you. That's very helpful." I shook my head. "But I have to go home. To my own family."

And to Jake, I thought. *I had to get back to Jake.*

Yami shrugged. "No worries. You'll ride with the postie. The postman."

I blinked. The mailman. Of course. I glanced over at my leotard, drying in the sun. "What time does he come?"

"Tuesday."

"Tuesday. But that was . . ."

Yami nodded. "Yesterday. He delivered the post right before the explosion. Right before you came."

"And he'll be back . . . ?"

"Next Tuesday."

Next Tuesday. Six days. I couldn't stay here six more days. I closed my eyes and collapsed backward into the sand. I'd battled Dracons and Bug fighters and paralyzing green beams, only to be defeated by the lonely Australian outback.

Marco would love this. Cassie the nature lover

finally gets out into nature and begs for technology.

A low buzzing hum pierced my thoughts. It started so softly I barely noticed it, then grew louder. It sounded like —

I sat up.

An airplane.

CHAPTER 17

I shielded my eyes against the sun. A small silver plane glinted on the horizon.

I raced from the lean-to and waved my arms over my head.

"Hey! Down here! Stop! STOP! Hey, down here!"

It was a small plane, flying low. It buzzed closer and closer and was now almost directly overhead.

"STO-O-O-O-O-OP!"

I jumped up and down in the sand, waving my arms like a crazed referee. Tjala bounded out of the lean-to and ran in circles around me, barking at the sky.

The pilot dipped his wing and flew on.

"HEY!"

I watched the plane grow smaller and smaller and disappear over the horizon. I was still holding my hands over my head. I let them drop to my sides.

"Tourists." Yami scratched Tjala's head. "You'll see them all morning flying in that direction, then all evening flying back the other way. Waving won't make them stop. They'll just snap pictures of the charming natives and fly on."

I wiped the sweat from my face and tried to catch my breath. The desert heat sucked the air right out of my lungs. "So where do they take off from? How far is it?"

"From the Alice. About one hundred kilometers from here."

One hundred kilometers. Okay. That was . . . what? We'd done this in math class. A kilometer was less than a mile, like maybe half a mile. Maybe a little more. So one hundred kilometers was only —

"Fifty or sixty miles." I stared out at the endless red desert. "Give or take a blistering acre or two."

Yami shook his head. "You'd never survive it," he said. "Not Cassie the girl. Cassie the bird, who knows? Too bad you aren't a kangaroo. A kangaroo could be making a telephone call in only a few hours." He laughed at his own joke.

"But even a kangaroo would wait till the sun went down."

He turned and walked back to his witchetty grub. Tjala followed. I stared at them.

A kangaroo. Fast. Smart. Built for the outback. Better than Crocodile Dundee with a big knife.

But could the kangaroo find its way to a pay phone? Because Cassie the girl sure couldn't, and she wouldn't have Yami along to lead her safely through the night desert.

I wiped my sticky neck on the sleeve of my T-shirt. Yami was right. I couldn't go anywhere till the sun went down. I would wait until nightfall, then morph kangaroo. Yami could give me directions to the nearest town. Just a few more hours and I would be on my way home.

I squinted up at the clear, bright sky. All I could do in the meantime was hope the Yeerks took a very long time organizing a search party.

A door slammed, and Yami's grandfather hobbled around the side of the house. His limp seemed worse than it had only a few minutes before. His hair was matted with sweat. When he reached the edge of Yami's porch, he stopped and leaned against it.

"Grandfather?" Yami set his bowl in the sand and ran toward the porch. I followed him.

Yami's grandfather pushed away from the

101

porch and stood upright. He held up a curved piece of dark wood. "For you," he told me. "You have given me a gift. And now I give a gift to you."

I took the wood. It was smooth and hard. "A boomerang," he said.

I opened my mouth. Nothing came out. I wanted to say I couldn't take it, that I didn't deserve it. I wanted to tell him the only things I'd given him were a broken radio antenna and exposure to an evil so absolute and terrifying that it had no place here in this untouched land.

I looked up. The old man's face burst into a smile. Yami's smile. I'd seen the same pure joy on Yami's face when he tried to share the witchetty grub.

The joy that turned to pain and embarrassment when I refused to eat them.

I ran my fingers over the boomerang. "Thank you," I said. "It's beautiful."

"Grandfather carves boomerangs and sends them to my aunt in the Alice," Yami said proudly. "Collectors buy them, and tourists, too, and art galleries even." He nodded at his grandfather. "Show her how to throw it."

Yami's grandfather smiled and nodded and led us around the trailer, steadying himself with one hand against the metal as he walked.

I leaned close to Yami. "Is he okay?" I whispered.

His grandfather waved a hand in the air without turning around. "I'm fine. I cut myself yesterday while carving. I've done it before." He laughed, but some of the thunder seemed to be missing from it. "You can be sure I'll do it again."

He led us to the edge of the outstation, away from the houses. He gripped one end of the boomerang in the palm of his hand and stood still for a moment, facing the wind. Then he pulled the boomerang back at his waist and hurled it sideways, low to the ground.

FFFFFwwwpppwwppppwwppp.

The boomerang shot over the desert, a deadly, spinning blur. It sliced a little pink flower off the top of a scrubby bush and skidded into the sand. Yami ran to get it. Tjala bounded after him.

"It doesn't come back?" I said.

"Yes, it comes back. As soon as Yami brings it." Yami's grandfather laughed. "This boomerang doesn't come back without help. Returning boomerangs are for games. I would throw a returning boomerang much differently, over my shoulder, like a ball. This is a hunting boomerang. A weapon."

Yami jogged back across the sand. I saw the

103

same natural ease I'd noticed when I'd first met him. Not like he was running across the desert, but like he was part of the desert. He smiled at me and wrinkled his eyes against the sun. "Your turn." He handed me the boomerang.

I took a deep breath and tried to stand the way his grandfather had. I pulled the boomerang back to my waist.

"No!" Yami reached toward me. "You have it backward."

I looked up as he looked down. Our noses brushed together.

"Oh."

"Sorry."

I stepped back in embarrassed confusion.

Yami turned away and looked at his feet. "My grandfather would be better at helping," he said.

I nodded and looked over at Yami's grandfather. He smiled weakly and started toward me. He stumbled. I caught his arm, and he sank against me.

"Grandfather!" Yami braced his other side, and we lowered him to the sand.

"Show me where you cut yourself," I said.

Yami's grandfather nodded and rolled up his pant leg. A putrid stench wafted out.

"Oh, man," I said.

A deep gash ran down his calf, from just below his knee to the middle of his shin. His leg was swollen and blistered, and the skin around the cut had turned purplish-black. I touched it. It was burning with fever. Pus oozed from the wound.

"You did this yesterday?" I said.

He nodded. "A new carving tool, sharper than anything." He dug into his pocket. "I found it in the desert. I saw it fall. It was a gift from the sky."

He held up a shard of metal, black and singed. My stomach jolted. It wasn't a gift.

It was a piece of the Bug fighter I'd shot down.

CHAPTER 18

The Bug fighter.

I stared at the charred black piece in his hand.

A hunk of metal. All the horrifying things that had happened over the last two days — all the horrifying things I'd done — had been because of a hunk of metal.

The Marines. The armored-truck guys. The Hork-Bajir. The Taxxon. And now Yami and his family, especially his grandfather, who had only wanted a good sharp tool to carve a boomerang. I had put every one of them in terrible danger.

Over a hunk of metal.

I stared at the injured leg. I'd helped my dad with a lot of injured animals, but I'd never seen an infection get this bad this fast.

Maybe I'd been wrong. Maybe a chunk of Bug fighter could spread weird alien diseases. Clearly the foreign metal had caused a horrible reaction in Yami's grandfather.

Whatever it was, we had to get the wound cleaned.

"Do you have a first-aid kit?" I asked.

Yami's grandfather nodded and lay back in the sand. "The medical kit and the natural medicines." He closed his eyes. "Yami's mother knows them all."

"Good. That's what we need for right now." I stared out at the desert. Heat shimmered up from the scrub. "But, Yami, we have to get him to a hospital. Somehow."

"There's the flying doctor," he said.

"The flying doctor?"

Yami nodded. "Not like the flying bird-girl." He tried to smile at his little joke but his chin quivered. "The Flying Doctor Service. They use airplanes to fly doctors over the outback."

"Like an ambulance in the air! But that's — that's exactly —" I stopped, my mouth open. "That's impossible, isn't it?"

Yami nodded.

We needed a radio to call the flying doctor. The radio I had destroyed.

"I can get my uncles to help us," he said.

Two of Yami's uncles carried his grandfather

107

inside. Yami's mother set a huge first-aid kit and a basket full of bottles and powders on a table by the bed.

She leaned over to examine the wound. "Oh!" She clapped her hand over her mouth and stared up at me. Fear filled her eyes.

"I know," I said.

The gash started on the inside of his calf, in the fleshy part below his knee, and curved down to his shin. Through pus I could see bone.

I helped Yami's mother clean the wound, then we left it uncovered to heal in the open air. Yami's mother gave his grandfather something to help him sleep, a natural drug from one of the desert shrubs. Then left us with him so she could go disinfect the things she'd used to clean the wound.

Yami and I sat next to the bed, watching his grandfather sleep. His chest rose in fits and shakes when he took in a breath, then fell with a shudder when he exhaled.

The floor of the house had been dug down into the ground. The dirt and stone walls kept it cooler than the desert outside. Still, the air in the tiny room was thick with heat and the stench of rotting flesh.

"Yami," I said, "he needs antibiotics. If I leave to get help now, the flying doctor could be here in a few hours."

Yami shook his head. "This is the middle of summer. You would never make it."

I mopped the sweat from his grandfather's face. "Do you remember what you said about changing into a kangaroo?"

He nodded.

"Well, I can do that. I can become a kangaroo, and I can get help."

He looked at me. "Do you remember the other thing I said? That even a kangaroo would wait till the sun went down? You wouldn't be able to travel very fast in this heat. You'd have to stop and rest and find shade." He narrowed his eyes. "And you wouldn't. You'd push yourself on. To get help. But you can't help my grandfather if, if —" His gaze flickered to the floor.

"If I die in the desert?"

He lifted his eyes. "Yes."

"Okay," I said. "I'll wait until sunset."

I didn't tell him I'd already planned to morph kangaroo and cross the desert during the night. My earlier panic about making a phone call suddenly seemed trivial.

We stayed with his grandfather all morning and into the afternoon. Yami's mother came in and out, and I helped her clean the wound and reapply the medicine.

It wasn't helping. The infection only grew.

Yami's mother left to gather more plants for

medicine. I sat on the floor with my back against the wall, waiting for nightfall. I leaned my head against the stone. I guess I closed my eyes.

"Hhhuuuuuhhhh."

A moan.

I blinked. Red streaks of light fell across the room. I glanced out the window. The sun was setting.

"Hhhhuuuuuuuuuhhhhh."

"Yami?" I stood up.

A hand clamped around my wrist.

"Aaahhhh!" I yelled.

It was Yami's grandfather. His hand was dry and burning with fever. He looked up at me. His eyes blazed in a bright frenzy against the gray of his face.

"Hhhhuh-hhhhelp me."

"I will. I am." I squeezed his hand between both of mine. "I'm going to get help."

I rubbed the back of his hand. He closed his eyes.

Then I glanced down at his wound.

"Oh, God."

His entire lower leg, from just under his knee to the top of his foot, was black and swollen like a basketball.

A throbbing, putrified basketball, about to explode.

CHAPTER 19

"Yami, wake up!"

Yami was leaning against the foot of the bed, his head on the mattress.

"Yami, we fell asleep. You have to wake up."

His dark head bobbed. "No worries. I am awake." He rubbed his eyes and climbed to his feet. Stared at his grandfather's leg. "Oh!"

"Yami, it's too late to get a doctor." I swallowed. "If we don't stop the infection — now — he'll die. And there's only one way we can stop it." I held his gaze with mine, so he would understand. "We have to get rid of it."

Yami nodded. Then the horror registered. "Get rid of . . . his leg."

"It will save his life, Yami. And once he's stable, I can go find a doctor."

"Yes. I'll get my mother." He ran out the door.

I sat on the edge of the bed and studied his grandfather's worn, rugged face. The old man's plea echoed through my head: *Help me.* Did he know what he was asking? Would he want to live with only one leg? Or would he rather we let him die?

But I knew the question was pointless. I wouldn't let him die when there was still something I could do to save him. I wouldn't let him suffer through the misery of being slowly eaten away by infection. I wouldn't let him go when there was still so much he needed to teach Yami.

I'd helped my dad with amputations — a deer, a coyote, a raccoon. All hit by cars. And I'd done surgery without my dad. Brain surgery, on Ax. It was the hardest thing I've ever done, but I'd do it again in a heartbeat. To save my friend's life.

One of my right choices, no doubt.

I patted the old man's hand and stood up. I needed a blade, a sharp blade, able to slice cleanly through a man's bone. And I knew where to get one.

I changed back into my leotard and concentrated.

Sschhoooooooop. Sschhoooooooop. Schoooop-schoop-schoop.

Blades erupted from my head, wrists, fore-arms, elbows. Everything else about me was still human. I was Cassie, the human switchblade.

And I could have stayed that way. I could have stopped the morph right there and used the blades to perform the operation. But I needed more than the blades. I needed the strength to use them, more strength than my young human arms possessed.

Ssscccrrrrruuuuuuuunnch.

My neck stretched up and out, a serpent neck extending from my shoulders. Shoulders that were bulging. Massive shoulders and arms pow-erful enough to wrench a full-grown oak from the ground. I grew taller. The blades on my serpent head scraped the ceiling.

Cccuuuuuurrrrrrreeeeeeeeekkkkkk.

My body dropped as my legs slammed back and up. My hips rotated and my knees reversed direction. My toes melded together and shot out into four claws on tyrannosaur feet.

Sshhhhrroooooooomp.

A thick tail shot out from the base of my spine and banged into the table, rattling the bottles of medicine. Skin grew thick and tough. Teeth, like scalpels, sprouted from my jaws.

I was Hork-Bajir. And not just any Hork-Bajir. I had two Hork-Bajir morphs now, but I had chosen to become the one I'd acquired on the airplane, the Hork-Bajir who had vaporized under the Dracon beam. I was a Xerox copy of a Hork-Bajir who could no longer exist except through the DNA in my blood.

And I was not a killer, not a natural terrorist for Visser Three. The Hork-Bajir was gentle, curious, and a little afraid. And he was going to help me save a life.

The door banged open, and I jumped.

"My mother is out in the desert. My aunt went to find —" Yami stared at me in horror. Backed against the wall.

<It's me,> I said. <I'm still Cassie. Here. Inside.> I clasped one fierce hand over my chest.

"Your voice." Yami pressed his hands against his ears.

<I know,> I said. <It's the best way for me to communicate with you right now.>

Yami pulled his hands down slowly. "You can save my grandfather like this?"

<Yes.>

He nodded. "Tell me how to help."

We scrubbed our hands, or, in my case, claws, and I disinfected my wrist blades. We elevated the infected leg with blankets, then Yami

114

gave his grandfather more of the pain medication his mother had made. Yami found a belt, and we used it as a tourniquet around his grandfather's thigh. This was tricky because I knew that the main artery lay deep within his leg.

I made a shallow incision below the knee, cutting only through the skin all the way around his leg.

I wiped my blade on a sterile gauze pad and took a deep breath. The air in the little room was boiling. The Hork-Bajir was not built for heat.

I let out the breath. <Okay, Yami, be ready, because there's going to be some blood.>

I needed to make one slice, clean and clear, straight through the muscle. A quick cut would cause the arteries to spasm and help control bleeding.

I positioned my blade over his leg. I slashed, down and around. The muscle fell neatly in half. Blood splurted from the vessel closest to the bone.

<There, Yami. That artery. Pinch it shut while I finish.>

Yami nodded. His lips went pale. He grabbed the artery with shaky fingers and squeezed.

I pushed the muscle back to reveal the two leg bones. One slice severed them both.

I demorphed quickly. Yami watched. His face

contorted in a silent scream, but he said nothing. He nearly collapsed with relief when my fully human form emerged.

I stitched the main arteries and veins, but left the skin flaps open. If I closed them now, the wound wouldn't drain, and infection would set in again. A doctor could stitch them closed when we got to a hospital.

Yami's grandfather stirred. His fever had broken. His face was drenched, but it had lost its deathly pallor.

He moaned and rolled his arm out over the edge of the bed. Something black and heavy clanked to the floor.

I picked it up. It was the chunk of Bug fighter.

As I stared at the metal, a shadow darkened the room. And I knew what it was before I looked out the window.

Visser Three's Blade ship hovered over the brush. A port on the bottom of the ship yawned open, and a Taxxon dropped out onto the red Australian plain.

CHAPTER 20

The Blade ship hung low in the sky, black and silent against the setting sun. An army of Taxxons and Hork-Bajir leaped from its belly. They spread out over the scrub, trampling bushes and grass. The Hork-Bajir were armed. They fired Dracon beams at anything that moved.

I leaned against the window. It was happening again. I'd led innocent people — Yami and his family — into danger.

His family!

I whirled. "Yami, where did your mother go?"

He motioned toward the door. "On the other side of the outstation, beyond the gum trees."

I nodded. "Good. Where's Tjala?"

Yami's eyes widened. He ran toward the door. "Tjala!"

The pup tore inside, wiggling and wagging.

<ANDALITE!> Visser Three's open thought-speak thundered through my head.

Yami pressed his hands over his ears. Tjala yelped and flattened himself against the floor.

<You didn't think I'd forget you, did you?> Pure evil penetrated my skull. <Surrender now, or I will annihilate every living thing within a square mile. You have three minutes.>

Three minutes. I stared out the window. I couldn't fight all those Taxxons and Hork-Bajir. Not alone.

And I couldn't hide. It would only put Yami and his family in more danger. Visser Three would kill them all just to flush me out.

I had to give him what he wanted. I had to come out in the open. If he saw me, he'd leave Yami's family alone. If he knew where I was, he wouldn't have to blast the desert into confetti looking for me.

One last Taxxon tumbled to Earth, then the port of the Blade ship rippled shut. The sky shimmered and the ship vanished, concealed behind a cloaking beam.

But Visser Three wasn't gone. He was hiding. Watching.

"They have no right to be here." Yami stood

behind me, watching the strange alien beings ransack his desert.

"They're here because of me."

"No." Yami's grandfather touched my arm.

I looked down, startled.

He drew a sharp breath. His face twisted in pain, but his eyes stayed bright and alert.

"They're here because they're evil." His voice was a low rasp. "You fight these creatures, yes?"

I nodded. "Yes."

"If you did not fight them, do you think they would leave us alone? Do you think they would stay away from this place and never hurt us? No. They would come. They would take our land, destroy our home. Our life would be gone forever. This I know." He swallowed. "Do everything you can, and anything you must." He closed his eyes. "I only wish I could help."

I touched his cheek. "You already have," I said.

<ANDALITE!> Visser Three's voice boomed. <Two minutes.>

I eased the door open and peered out into the shadows. Nothing. I slipped onto the porch.

I needed strength, speed, and endurance. A morph that was desert-ready. I focused on kangaroo.

Crrreeeaaaacccckkkk!

My hips swung forward. Thighs bulged into

hulking mounds of muscle. My feet shot out, longer than my forearms. Toenails thickened and stretched. The two middle toes on each foot melted into one solid, claw-tipped bayonet.

Shhhhuuuuuuurrooooooomp.

A tail shot from my spine, a column of pure muscle, as long as the rest of my body and as thick as my neck. The skin on my belly stretched to form a pouch.

Ssssccuuuuuuuuurrrunnch.

My skull shifted back and out as my nose and jawbone sprouted into a muzzle. Ears stretched and shot to the top of my head. Dense fur spread from my whiskers to the tip of my tail.

<ANDALITE! ONE MINUTE.>

I was Information Central, sensing everything at once.

My eyes peered through the long shadows on the porch, picking up the slight movement of grass twisting in the wind.

My ears flicked and twitched. I could turn them in any direction, like two satellite dishes, tuning into the scuffing sound of Taxxon belly scraping against sand.

I sniffed. The sweet sharp scent of some desert plant mingled with the wretched odor of Hork-Bajir. I shuffled to the edge of the porch, using my tail as a prop while I balanced on my front feet and swung my back legs forward.

I spotted the boomerang lying on the bench. The boomerang Yami's grandfather had given me. I reached for it. The kangaroo's front paws were amazing, almost like hands, without a real thumb, but with five nimble, clawed fingers. I gripped the boomerang in one paw, held my pouch open with the other, and slipped the boomerang inside.

<ANDALITE! Your time is up.>

Bummmph. Bummmph. I leaped out onto the open sand.

CHAPTER 21

Bummmph. Bummmph.

I hopped between the houses of the little settlement. My nose twitched. Foul Taxxon breath drifted toward me on the desert wind.

One of the Hork-Bajir looked up. Then a Taxxon. One by one the Yeerks stopped combing the desert and watched me.

I stood upright, ears flicking, ready to make my move. A gunfighter facing off against a gang of outlaws.

I had to let the Yeerks know I was the Andalite bandit, not just a misguided kangaroo. And then I had to run as fast as I could for as long as I could and lead them as far away as I could.

Bummmph. Bummmph. Bummmph.

I leaped to the edge of the settlement and faced the empty spot in the sky where the Blade ship had vanished.

I could almost hear Rachel: "Let's do it!"

And Marco: "Are you insane?"

Maybe, I said silently. No.

<ANDALITE!>

TSEEEEEEEEEWWWWWWWW!

The ground exploded at my feet.

I bolted. My legs were like coiled springs.

Bummph. I landed on both feet.

I leaped again, soaring what felt like the length of an eighteen-wheeler, my tail curved out behind me for balance.

Taxxon and Hork-Bajir-Controllers crunched through the scrub behind me. I veered off, away from the settlement, away from the clump of gum trees and Yami's mother.

Bummmph. Bummmph. Bummmph.

The tendons at the backs of my legs were like rubber bands. I landed, and the rubber band shot me back into space. The faster I hopped, the more energy I had. I could leap forever.

TSEEEEEEEEEWWWWWWWW!

A Hork-Bajir jumped out ahead of me.

I turned.

TSEEEEEEEEEWWWWWWWW!

Another Hork-Bajir and a Taxxon.

I whirled. Another Taxxon, dead ahead. He

123

slithered toward me, his centipede legs shooting him across the sand.

I leaped! He lunged! Hundreds of Taxxon pincers, like lobster claws, latched onto my fur.

I raked at him with my front paws. His pincers held tight, pulling me closer, closer. His Jell-O eyes quivered. Drool spilled from his mouth. His razor teeth slammed together like a guillotine, an inch above my neck. I leaned back, supporting my kangaroo body on the muscled coil of my tail, and kicked.

THUMP! Thwuump-thwuump.

The massive muscles that had propelled me across the desert now released their force on the Taxxon. My back legs struck, again and again. I shredded him with my dagger claws. He sank back from me, Taxxon goo oozing onto the sand.

More Taxxons swarmed toward us. I turned and leaped away. The Taxxons let me go.

Their rabid hunger zeroed in on their mangled comrade. The Yeerks inside their heads powerless to stop them. The Taxxons ripped into their fallen colleague. The wounded Taxxon himself turned and, with his last dying breath, slurped up his own guts.

Their little snack break bought me some time. I bounded across the scrub, surrounded on three sides. Taxxons and Hork-Bajir behind me and to my left. The settlement and grove of gum trees to my right. Only one way lay open, directly in front of me: the spring.

The Yeerks had already trampled Yami's homeland and terrified his family. Now I was leading them to the sacred spring of his ancestors.

My choice. I had to get them as far away from Yami and his family as I could.

The Taxxons had finished feeding and were now slithering after me. Most of the Hork-Bajir had fallen behind. The desert was an oven, even with the sun going down. Their heavy Hork-Bajir bodies couldn't take the heat.

But they were still armed.

TSEEEEEEEEEWWWWWWWWW!

The sand exploded under me.

TSEEEEEEEEEEWWWWWWWWW!

A bush burst into flames.

I kept hopping. The ground sloped downward. The scrub became thicker. Ahead lay the spring.

And in front of it, between me and the water, a group of large animals grazed in the grass.

No! I couldn't believe it. I'd led the Yeerks right to the kangaroos.

One of the 'roos, a female, bounded toward me, her joey bouncing along in her pouch. I recognized her. She was the doe I had untangled from the fence.

My own kangaroo's identical twin.

125

CHAPTER 22

TSEEEEEEEEWWWWWWWWW!

A crater erupted at the edge of the spring.

The kangaroos scattered, thundering over the grass. Bummmph. Bummmph. They hopped in every direction, looping back and forth, surrounding me.

TSEEEEEEEEWWWWWWWWW!

A boomer fell at my feet. The stench of burning fur filled the desert.

I had to break free. The Yeerks were firing at anything that moved. They didn't know which kangaroo was me!

I leaped away from the spring, toward the open desert.

Most of the female kangaroos had scattered

across the plain, but the males, the big boomers, didn't move as fast as the does. They were twice as big. And twice as heavy.

Two of them were locked in combat with a Hork-Bajir, swiping with their claws as he slashed with his blades. Another lay on the grass, unmoving. Ravenous Taxxons descended upon him.

One of the boomers leaped toward the water. Another followed. And another.

They looked like they were fleeing, backing themselves into a watery corner in their panic to get away. Taxxons scrambled toward the spring in frenzied anticipation. They didn't know the boomers were leading them into a trap.

Or trying to.

I turned back toward the spring. The boomers were fighting my battle, and I couldn't let them fight alone. I leaped into the water.

The doe I'd rescued stood on the shore. <Go,> I said. She watched me. She sniffed her pouch. Then she turned and hopped away.

I kicked toward deeper water. My entire body was submerged except for the uppermost curve of my rump and the top of my head — eyes, ears, the long ridge of my muzzle, nose. Powerful hind legs paddled, moving almost as well in water as on land.

More Taxxons slipped into the spring behind

me. The Hork-Bajir followed, splashing in to the tops of their talons. Then they stopped. Couldn't go any further. Their dense, tree-climbing bodies would sink in the mud at the bottom of the spring.

So they raised their Dracon beams instead.

TSEEEEEEW-buh-LOOOOOOSH!

A blast shot over my head. Heat singed my ears.

TSEEEEEEW-buh-LOOOOOOSH!

Water boiled around me.

Taxxons motored toward us. Their lobster claws propelling them headlong into the waiting roos.

The Taxxons lunged. The kangaroos threw their heads back and clawed. Pulled the bloated Taxxons down in the water!

A Taxxon barreled down on me, backing me toward the cliff. Another circled and came at me from behind. Claws snatched at me, front and back. I raked and kicked. The Taxxons pressed in. Pushed me under!

I fought to keep my face above the surface. Leaned back. Water lapped into my ears. A slurping Taxxon mouth bore down on me. My ears slipped under, then my eyes. My muzzle. My mouth. Only the tip of my nose remained above the water.

The Taxxon lunged. I kicked. Slashed! The

water churned around me. My nose buried in foul Taxxon flesh! The Taxxon was on top of me now, pushing me down. I plunged deeper and deeper into the cool bottom water.

I struggled to break free. Taxxon claws, locked onto my fur, pressing down, down. Thrashing . . . legs and shoulders dragged through the water. Lungs burning!

I dug my paws into the Taxxon's skin. His fat body bobbed like a beach ball. I pulled my hind legs up and around, so that I was on my back, under the Taxxon.

Schloooomp. Schloooomp.

I kicked. My middle toes plunged into the soft flesh of the Taxxon's belly.

Spuh-LOOOOOOSH.

The Taxxon exploded! Popped like a big, nasty pimple.

The force of the eruption propelled me to the surface. Air! I sucked in lungfuls of air. The other Taxxons writhed toward the site like maggots.

I jetted away from them.

TSEEEEEEW-buh-LOOOOOOSH!

The water sizzled.

I whirled. A Hork-Bajir aimed at my head.

TSEEEEEEW-buh-LOOOOOOSH!

I dodged.

TSEEEEEEW-buh-LOOOOOOSH!

I dove.

The Hork-Bajir raised his weapon again.

FFFFFwwwpppwwppppwwppp.

A whirling blur whipped over my head. A boomerang! It struck the Hork-Bajir in the throat, knocking him backward into the grass. His serpent neck was sliced nearly in half.

I turned. Yami and his uncles were above me, crouched on the rocky bluff of the cliff.

CHAPTER 23

FFFFFwwwpppwwppppwwppp. FFFFFwwwpppwwppppwwppp.

The men of the outstation launched a
squadron of boomerangs.

Thup. Thup.

Two more Hork-Bajir fell.

"Harr gurfass!" A Hork-Bajir pointed at the
cliff.

The others raised their Dracon beams.

<Yami! Get out of here!> I screamed in
thought-speak. <You'll be killed!>

TSEEEEEEEEWWWWWWWW!

The edge of the cliff exploded.

<Yami!>

131

"No worries!" Yami's voice rang out over the spring.

FFFFFwwwpppwwppppwwppp.   FFFFFwww-pppwwppppwwppp.

Another Hork-Bajir fell.

TSEEEEEEEEEWWWWWWWW!

The Dracon beam blasted a cave into the wall of the cliff.

I kicked toward the shore. Had to show Visser Three I was the Andalite bandit! Had to lead the Yeerks away from Yami and his family!

Other kangaroos swam past me. They had clawed most of the Taxxons to shreds. The remaining two or three aliens were busy devouring their dying brothers. The boomers sloshed ashore and leaped toward the open desert.

I climbed from the water near the cliff.

TSEEEEEEEEEWWWWWWWW!

The rock wall exploded above my head. I dodged. A Hork-Bajir bounded toward me.

"RUFF! Grrrrrrrr!"

A dog! Tjala scrambled down the cliff and vaulted for the Hork-Bajir. The Hork-Bajir spun.

<Tjala, no!> I bounded toward them.

The Hork-Bajir aimed his Dracon at Tjala. I leaned back on my tail and kicked. Bone hit blade.

TSEEEEEEEEEWWWWWWWW!

The Dracon fired out over empty desert.

I dropped to the sand. My tail lay in two pieces, severed by the Hork-Bajir's knee blade. Jagged bone pierced through the skin of my thigh.

The Hork-Bajir turned. Watched me twist in agony. Drew up to his full height and leveled his weapon.

"Grrrrrrrrrrrrrrrrrr."

Tjala leaped. The Hork-Bajir fired. Tjala clamped his jaws over the weapon.

TSEEEEEEEEWWWWWWWW!

A sapling behind me exploded. The Hork-Bajir stumbled and fell to the ground. The Dracon beam skidded across the sand.

Tjala turned, teeth bared.

"Grrrrrrrrrrrrrrrrrrrrrr."

He lunged! Ripped into the Hork-Bajir. Knew to go for the throat. Clamped his jaws on the alien's neck.

The Hork-Bajir lashed out. Flung his serpent's head from side to side. Wrist blades sliced through the air an inch above Tjala's back.

The Hork-Bajir twisted sideways and pushed up with his arms. Whipped his head. Tjala's grip broke, and he fell backward into the scrub. The Hork-Bajir climbed to his feet. He wiped his palm across his neck and looked at the blood.

133

Tjala barked. The Hork-Bajir stood frozen for a moment, looking first at Tjala, then his bloody hand.

The Hork-Bajir turned and ran away.

Tjala bounded over to me. He licked my muzzle and sniffed my bleeding tail.

<Good . . . boy . . . Tjala.>

I needed a hiding place. Had to demorph. Soon. I closed my front claw around a clump of grass and pulled myself toward one of the boulders at the base of the cliff.

Bzzzzzzzzzzzzzzzz.

A low droning, almost like a mosquito, buzzed in the distance. Tjala barked at the sky. I turned my head.

A glint of silver flashed on the horizon. Then another. I watched. Two tourist planes were headed directly toward us.

Visser Three must have seen them, too. His thought-speak boomed over the battlefield. <Human aircraft approaching. Retreat. NOW! Reboard and prepare for cleanup. These human pilots WILL NOT see evidence of this battle.>

The sky shimmered, and the bottom of the Blade ship appeared. The port rippled open. Hork-Bajir leaped and hobbled toward the ship. Drop shafts descended to suck them up into the port.

Two beams shot down from the front of the

ship and scanned the desert floor, zapping each remnant of the battle.

All evidence of Yeerk presence sizzled and vanished. Handheld Dracons, fallen Hork-Bajir, the floating carcass of a half-eaten Taxxon.

The drop shafts rose back up into the belly of the ship, the sky rippled again, and the Blade ship disappeared. All that remained were the craters they'd blasted into the desert. And dozens of boomerangs scattered through the scrub.

Yami and his uncles cheered. Tjala barked and scrambled up the cliff toward them.

The two tourist planes buzzed overhead. Both pilots dipped their wings at the charming natives and flew on.

I collapsed behind the boulder.

"Cassie, you must demorph quickly."

<Aaah!>

I jerked my head around and rammed my nose into something hard. A leg. A canine-shaped leg of ivory and steel. I looked up. A Chee towered over me. A Chee I recognized.

<Lour — Lourdes?>

"Yes." A shimmer and her human hologram slipped into place. "I smuggled aboard the Blade ship. I'm here to get you home."

<Home.> I closed my eyes.

"Home." Lourdes's voice sounded so soothing. She was taking me home. I would be safe.

"Your people have been searching for you night and day. You chose a very good place to hide."

I opened my eyes. <Hide? You saw . . . the outstation?>

"The little group of houses back there? Yes."

<There's a man . . . he needs . . . doctor. Call . . . flying doctor.>

"Flying doctor. Okay. I've got it covered. You just morph back. I've extended a hologram around the boulder. No one can see you."

I nodded and closed my eyes.

CHAPTER 24

"Consumerism completely baffles you, doesn't it, Cassie?" Rachel dropped her bag on the table.

We were at The Gardens, the combination wildlife and amusement park where my mom works. Rachel and I had just come from the bathroom. Jake, Marco, Tobias, and Ax were waiting for us in the main concession area. Tobias and Ax were both in human morph. Ax was eyebrow deep in a box of popcorn.

Rachel slumped into the chair next to Tobias. "Can you imagine my elation, my total euphoria, when Cassie, OUR Cassie, said she wanted to go shopping?"

Marco nodded. "You were expecting to lay down serious cash at the mall."

"Exactly! See?" She turned to me. "Even Marco understands." She shook her head. "But no, Cassie drags me to the zoo — the ZOO — where she ransacks the gift shop and comes up with a postcard. A POSTCARD. Cassie, buying a postcard at the zoo is not shopping. Say it with me now. Postcard. Zoo. Not. Shopping."

I shrugged, hoping to look casual, and slid into the chair across from Jake.

He dipped a fry in his ketchup. "What kind of postcard?"

I knew he'd ask me that. I smiled, casually, and reached into my bag. "It's just something I wanted." I glanced down to make sure I was pulling out the right card. "A reminder."

I held it up. It was a red kangaroo, a doe, with a joey peeking out of her pouch.

"Hey!" Marco reached across and took the card from me. "It's Cassie in her other life. Hop-a-long Cassie-dee."

"Yeah." Tobias smiled at me, his strange, un-blinking Hawk-boy smile. "The one where she doesn't need the rest of us. The one where she single-handedly defeats all alien life-forms from here to Sydney."

"Sydney!" I thumped my head. "Of course. SYD."

Rachel looked at me. "SYD?"

I nodded. "All the baggage tags said SYD. I couldn't figure it out. Duh. They were going to Sydney, Australia."

"Well, yeah," said Tobias, "they were. Unfortunately, most of them didn't make it."

"Yeah, Cassie." Marco dropped a nacho into his mouth. "Some rich old Australian guy is offering a bundle of cash for information leading to the arrest and conviction of the person or persons responsible for stealing a sweater and two bottles of prune juice from his suitcase." He wiped cheese from his chin. "You wouldn't happen to know anything about that, would you? I'm thinking we might have a real chance at the reward money."

"What is he doing?" Rachel frowned at Ax, who was now leaning back in his chair with the empty popcorn box mashed over his face.

"What do you think he's doing?" Marco grabbed the box. "Ax-man. Cardboard isn't one of the major food groups, remember?"

Ax sucked the butter off his fingers. "Unfortunately I am not in another morph. Or I would be able to reach the last bit of grease and salt with my tongue."

Marco rolled his eyes. "I'll buy you another box. And here, clean your face off." He threw Ax a wad of napkins. "Do I need to start carrying baby wipes for you?"

I watched Marco and Ax walk toward the concession stand. Took a deep breath. "I've been wondering" — I wasn't sure I even wanted to ask this — "does anybody know, I mean, did anybody see —"

"What happened to the Marines?" Jake asked.

I nodded. "Yeah. How did you — ?"

He shrugged. "You're you, Cassie. Anyway, the official story is a UA. Unauthorized Absence. The Marine Corps says two Marines hijacked an armored truck loaded with sensitive Defense Department research."

"Translation: Bug fighter wreckage," said Tobias.

"Right," Jake agreed. "The Marines, the truck, and the guys who were supposed to be driving the truck all disappeared into the mountains. The Marines dropped the armored-truck guys off in the parking lot of some roadside tourist attraction —"

"World's biggest ball of gum wrappers." Rachel.

"And nobody's seen the Marines or the truck since." Jake sighed. "So, I guess that one was a tie. NASA doesn't have the chunk of Bug fighter, but neither do the Yeerks."

He smiled at me. He'd been sitting with one hand wrapped around his Coke, and now he laid it flat on the table so that his fingertips were touching mine. He looked into my eyes. A little flip of hair fell down over his eyebrow. "Except you're back now, Cassie. So we won. We definitely won."

I turned his hand over and squeezed it. He squeezed back.

He glanced sideways at Rachel and Tobias, then leaned toward me and lowered his voice. "I was kind of hoping we could hang out. You know, to talk."

"Talk?" Rachel rolled her eyes. "Puh-leez. He wants to give you a big, fat, sloppy kiss. You should've seen him. He was a total zombie the whole time you were gone."

I smiled at Jake. "A zombie? Really?"

Jake shot Rachel a dirty look, then stared down at his french fries. "Depends on your definition of a zombie."

"How's this for a definition?" Tobias said. "Somebody who can't eat, can't sleep, spends every minute of the night and day searching the airport and all other known Yeerk hangouts, and can only utter one intelligible sentence: 'I have to FIND HER.'"

Jake rolled his eyes. "Okay, so I was a zombie."

He looked up at me and smiled. A little ball of guilt wedged itself in my throat. While Jake had

141

been ripping the city apart looking for me, I'd been taking boomerang lessons from somebody else. What kind of person was I?

I looked past Jake. Marco and Ax were weaving their way through the tables, loaded down with greasy, salty snacks.

Marco set another plate of nachos on the table. He looked at Jake, then me. "Uh, is *the* moment over now? Because some of us would like to eat."

Ax picked the kangaroo postcard up from the table so he'd have a place for his popcorn and his onion blossom.

"Cassie, it is good to have you back," he said. "Erek the Chee projects an excellent hologram but it could never take your place."

I smiled. "Thanks, Ax. And speaking of Erek, next time he fills in for me he needs to turn his brilliance down a notch. He aced my algebra test, and now my parents think I'm some kind of math genius. My mom wants to enroll me in accelerated calculus next semester. She says I haven't been living up to my potential."

"Your mother can't even imagine how infinite your potential is," Rachel commented.

Ax studied the postcard in his hand. "You were an animal with two heads?"

"No, Ax, that other head belongs to the baby

kangaroo. See? The mother carries him in her pouch. You know, like a pocket."

"A baby in a pocket." Ax frowned at the postcard, then handed it to me. "Is it effective?"

"Amazingly effective, Ax." I slipped the card into my sack, on top of the other card. The card even Rachel hadn't seen. The card that had taken me forever to find. I'd practically turned the rack upside down and shaken it. But I'd found it. An osprey in full flight.

Later, I addressed it when I was in the bathroom waiting for Rachel: Piti Spring Community, Northern Territory, Australia. I didn't sign it. Yami would know. I would mail it from the airport. I figured an airport postmark was pretty anonymous. Untrackable. Even for Visser Three.

The message was short: No worries.

#45 The Revelation

We ordered burgers from an all-night diner on the outskirts of town. The place was too much of a dump for the Yeerks to check out. I hoped. I made us eat in the car anyway, in a dark corner of the parking lot.

I told Dad everything. Almost.

My story seemed to wash over him somehow. He looked stunned, disbelieving. He shook his head as though everything I was telling him was, well, just too much for the man.

When I stopped talking, the first thing he said was that he had to call Nora.

I let him walk across the gravel parking lot to the pay phone. Let him dial the numbers.

"Honey, it's me," he said. "Yeah, I'm okay."

I could hear Nora on the other end. Yelling, worried, scared.

"I'm with Marco," Dad said. "Where? We're at the . . ."

I cut the connection and grabbed the receiver from Dad's ear. Slammed it down angrily.

He glared at me. "What was that!" he demanded.

For the first time since the brutality at Russ's house, it felt like the father I knew was with me. Real Dad. Thinking Dad. Authority-figure Dad. For the first time since I'd demorphed, the look in his eye was anything but distant.

"Why did you do that!"

I started to walk back to the car. He followed.

"I said, what was that about!"

I sat down on the passenger car seat. Dad got in his side and slammed the door. He had a door to slam.

"You know exactly what it was about," I said calmly. "If you've been listening to me at all, you know that by now the Yeerks have staked out our house, probably tapped our phone. I'd bet they're sitting on our couch right now, waiting for you to walk in the door so they can . . ."

"Stop," Dad said angrily. "Stop it. I've listened to you. I've heard every word. But you have to understand . . . I have no proof, no . . . how can I believe all these things you say? You changed from a gorilla into my son. But I only think I saw that. I was terrified. I was tortured, then kidnapped. Maybe my mind is making things up. Maybe this is a dream."

Before he'd finished talking, I was on my way.

My skin hardened, then blackened, then thinned like eggshell. Legs and arms shortened until there was nothing left to hold me up. I fell forward onto the seat, shrinking and shrinking until the crumbs from the burger bun looked like boulders, and then blindness cut my view.

Shlooooop!

My waist reduced to millimeters, splicing me almost in half.

"Oh, God!" Dad cried. "Oh, no!"

I was becoming an ant. But I wasn't going to wait for the ant's un-mind to surface. No.

I began to demorph.

I let Dad watch me, and all the horror and weirdness of morphing. I let Dad sit there, alone and up close with his new reality, as I demorphed back to boy. And began to morph again.

Feathers imprinted my skin in 2-D, then 3-D. They grew up and out as my body shrank and my head deformed. My nose grew hard and sharp and hooked. My fingers, though smaller, grew stronger, became flesh-piercing talons. Eyes sharpened to superhuman clarity.

Again, I started the return trip to boy. Back to the form Dad knew as his son.

"I have about twenty other animals I could morph to," I said as the last feather disappeared. "Want to see my lobster?"

A cold sweat coursed in tiny rivulets down the side of my father's head. He didn't need to see any more.

I'd scared him, creeped him out. Made him nervous and worried and concerned. He was handling it. For a guy whose reality had just been completely rocked, he was handling it pretty well.

He looked out through the windshield and stared for a moment at a point far away. The sun was just beginning to think about rising. It gave our desolate patch of the world a preview. Dad looked back at me.

"I get it," he said slowly. "I get it. You've been through hell."

"Through hell and back." I smiled. "A few times."

Dad smiled back.

"I'm going to take you to some friends of mine, Dad," I said. "You can hang out with them until we decide . . ."

"Whoa," Dad said quickly. "Are you nuts? I'm going to the police."

"Dad, the Yeerks are the police. I can't let you do that."

He was shocked and confused again. "What do you mean you can't let me. *I'm* your father. I tell *you* what to do."

Not in this reality, Dad. Not in this world.

"Dad, of course you're my father," I said, fighting an onslaught of emotion. And it would be so nice to have someone make decisions for me again, I added silently. "I love you. I respect you. But I've been fighting this war for a long time. I've been on more missions, in more fights, and seen more terrible things than you can imagine. This is my fight. My war. Me and my friends, we know what's going on. You don't. . . ."